THE DRAGON'S WEAKNESS

Tahoe Dragon Mates #5

JESSIE DONOVAN

Mythical Lake Press, LLC

This book is a work of fiction. Names, characters, places, and incidents are either the product of the writer's imagination or are used fictitiously, and any resemblance to actual persons, living or dead, business establishments, events, or locales is entirely coincidental.

The Dragon's Weakness
Copyright © 2021 Laura Hoak-Kagey
Mythical Lake Press, LLC
First Print Edition

Cover Art by Laura Hoak-Kagey of Mythical Lake Design
ISBN: 978-1944776978

Books in this series:

Tahoe Dragon Mates

∽

The Dragon's Weakness Synopsis

Dragon-shifter leader of Clan StoneRiver, David Lee, has vowed to never take a mate. The previous five clan leaders all lost their mates to tragedy, and he is determined to prevent any other female from sharing the same fate. Even when he discovers his true mate is human, David tries his best to keep his distance to protect her. But when he's forced to be near Tiffany for a week, during an event to help orphaned dragon-shifter children, the human becomes harder to resist. It's going to take everything he has to keep her safe.

Tiffany Ford is thrilled to be selected to help with the orphaned dragon children. Even if the StoneRiver clan leader is distant and borderline rude to her at first, she soon makes friends and enjoys herself. When David sets her a surprising challenge to test her observation skills, she's intrigued. And never one to back down, she accepts, curious to discover more about the leader.

As the days go by, Tiffany starts to realize there is more to David than his aloofness, making her wonder if there could be something between them. The only problem is that they both have doubts about each other. Will they be able to move past them before it's too late? Or will a sudden enemy take away their chance at a happy future forever?

NOTE: This is a quick, steamy standalone story about fated mates and sexy dragon-shifters near Lake Tahoe in the USA. You don't have to read all my other dragon books to enjoy this one!

Chapter One

David Lee didn't think of himself as a coward. After all, he'd been leader of Clan StoneRiver for nearly a decade and had dealt with would-be terrorists, the American Department of Dragon Affairs, and even other clans trying to encroach on his territory. Pressure and even danger wasn't anything new to him.

However, as he watched the volunteers for the week-long dragon orphans event arriving, he was tempted to hide in a corner to avoid one particular female.

His inner dragon—the second personality inside his head—sighed. *I think it's admirable she wants to help. She's human, and yet she's volunteering her time to help the orphan dragon children.*

Except you're forgetting one very important thing, dragon

—you know she's our true mate. That's reason enough I need to avoid her.

His beast grunted. *You're the only one who has a problem with that. I want her, and if she shows the tiniest bit of interest, I'll kiss her.*

No, you won't. I'm stronger and I'll stop you.

His dragon huffed and fell silent. When it came to control of their mind, David was indeed stronger.

Well, as long as he didn't kiss the human female and start the mate-claim frenzy. His dragon would then take over, David unable to halt the instinctual need, and his beast would stop at nothing to fuck the human until she was pregnant.

And David couldn't let that happen, not even if the female in question wanted it. Hell, wanted *him*.

No, because any female who became his mate would, in effect, be receiving a death sentence. And that wasn't something he wanted on his conscience.

His dragon sighed. *Not this again.*

Deny it all you like, but the last five StoneRiver clan leaders have all lost their mates within the first few years of claiming them. I won't risk any female's life that way.

There's no fucking curse.

You might not believe that, but what about the assholes who target dragon-shifters and want to banish them to other countries? They're a threat. And make no mistake—they'll target any mate of ours, if they can.

They've been quiet.

That doesn't mean they don't exist.

David was all too aware of the America for Humans Only League—AHOL—who would like nothing more than to banish every last dragon-shifter from the United States, whatever it took.

The League had caused trouble for the human mate of one of his clan members nearly a year ago. It was only a matter of time before they tried something else.

Especially if David did indeed take a human mate himself. The League viewed humans mated to dragon-shifters as dirty traitors. While the League had avoided killing anyone for a while, at least to his knowledge, they'd done so in the past and would no doubt do it again.

And given the history of Clan StoneRiver, the odds were that a kidnapping and maybe even murder would happen to any mate of his.

Before his dragon could try to argue yet again why they should woo Tiffany Ford—their true mate —some of the volunteers arrived, and he smiled as he greeted them.

Most of them were dragon-shifters, but humans either mated to a dragon or related to a human who was had been able to apply to help.

Which meant Tiffany, whose brother was mated to a female dragon-shifter on nearby Clan PineRock, had every right to be here.

His beast sighed. *More than a right. Her essay, for why she wanted to help, was easily the best of them all.*

Not wanting to remember her passionate, kind words and how she'd wished to take in all the children herself, if she could, David ignored his beast and kept an eye on the door. As the minutes ticked by and she didn't show, he wondered if maybe Tiffany wouldn't come after all.

He didn't wish anything bad to happen to her, but if she just so happened to catch a cold and had to stay home, the next week would be so much easier.

Especially since she'd never come to StoneRiver, and he rarely ventured to the bar and restaurant owned by one of his clan members, where Tiffany worked.

So yes, if she didn't come this week, David would probably be able to avoid her for a long time, if not forever.

Which meant she'd be safe. And even if he didn't really know her, that was important to him. Protecting his clan was paramount, and it was easy enough to extend that drive to the true mate he could never have.

And as the clock ticked ever closer to the end of the registration period with no sign of the female, he decided the next week might not be so bad after all.

TIFFANY FORD SCOWLED at the retreating car. Her older brother Ryan had lectured her for twenty minutes about the need to be careful and watch her back.

As if she didn't know that already.

But any attempt to remind her brother that she worked part-time at the human-dragon bar near StoneRiver—which meant she was more than aware of how to handle dragon-shifters and how to spot their enemies by now—had been quickly dismissed.

Even though she was twenty-seven and had more than enough common sense to be called an adult, her brother would always see her as his much younger sister, meaning she needed protection and guidance.

Funny, that, considering she'd been the one to help him move past the betrayal of his awful ex-wife, which had resulted in him finding his dragon-shifter mate, a woman who was as besotted with Ryan as he was with her.

Once the car was out of sight, she half walked, half jogged toward the main building. She'd been looking forward to the start of camp for weeks. While her job overseeing a variety of activities for the children would be fun, she was most hopeful about the larger events, the ones where prospective adopters were coming to meet the children. Most of whom had been abandoned with little more than a note, almost all of the orphans half-human.

And since the gene to shift into a dragon was always dominant, even half-human children had to live with a dragon clan.

Apparently, too many human mothers hadn't wanted to do that.

Even though Tiffany knew there were all kinds of circumstances that could lead to the heartbreaking decision, it still made her heart ache for the abandoned children. She wished she could adopt them all. But not only was that unrealistic for so many reasons, but she was also merely a human, and the DDA would never allow her to raise a dragon-shifter child on her own. Maybe if she had a dragon mate, it would be a different story.

But Tiffany didn't. And she wasn't entirely sure if she'd ever have either a dragon mate or a human husband.

Not wanting to think about all the reasons she was cynical when it came to love despite what she'd done for her brother, she jogged the last few feet until she reached the entrance to the main building. Taking a deep breath, she smoothed her hair, gripped her duffel bag tighter in her hand, and went inside.

The reception area consisted of a large, wide-open space with three tables side by side to form one long line at the far end. Both familiar and unfamiliar faces sat at the tables, behind various piles of paper and pamphlets.

And behind them all stood StoneRiver's clan leader, David Lee.

Even though she lived with another dragon clan —PineRock—she'd met the StoneRiver leader once or twice. He'd always been curt and cool, almost running to get away from her as soon as possible.

However, this time he merely stood with his hands clasped behind his back and stared at her.

As she walked closer toward the tables, she noticed his eyes were so dark they were nearly black. And yet, when his pupils flashed from round to slitted, she could easily see the change.

He was older than her, and taller, and extremely attractive with his broad shoulders, firm mouth, and dark hair. His golden-skinned, muscled biceps—one of which had a dragon tattoo on it—only added to his overall sexiness.

Not that she should notice any of that, especially since all dragonmen seemed to be sexy in their own way. Yes, partly due to looks, but also because most of them radiated a confidence few humans could match.

But David was a clan leader—and from what she'd heard working at the bar from her boss, Tasha —he was against ever taking a mate. So he was most definitely a look-but-don't-touch sort of dragonman.

Still, he was the main person in charge and could've denied her application, but he hadn't. He may be indifferent to her, but she'd at least be kind. Surely if he put on this event to help find parents for orphans, he couldn't be entirely awful.

Walking up to the area where he stood, she smiled and said, "Hello, Mr. Lee."

The dragonwoman sitting in front of him snorted. Tiffany recognized the brown-haired, blue-eyed woman as Megan Lee—the sister to her employer's mate. The woman said, "Since when do people call you Mr. Lee, David?"

He shrugged. "I never said she had to."

Oh, great. She'd tried to be polite, but somehow, it'd backfired.

Maybe she should've listened more closely to the various pieces of advice her in-laws and even PineRock's leader had given her over the last few weeks concerning tips about how to talk with the StoneRiver clan members. If only she'd thought to record the advice to listen to again later, she might remember it better in the present. "Well, I didn't know if you go by David, Dave, Davey, or any other number of nicknames. I know people try to call me Tiffy, and it takes everything I have not to wince. I'm not a dog or six years old."

His face remained impassive. "David is fine."

She nodded and put out a hand. "It's nice to see you again, David. Maybe I'll run into you again over the course of the week."

He looked at her hand, his pupils flashed, and he nodded.

But he didn't shake.

Tiffany had heard good things about StoneRiver's leader, but she was starting to think he might not be as nice as everyone had said he was.

Taking her hand back, she focused on Megan, who gave David a strange look before handing over Tiffany's welcome information and explained a few things about the schedule for the week.

David may have refused to shake, but from the corner of her eyes, she could see him still staring at her.

Maybe he was a broody dragonman, like some sort of hero in one of the romance books she read. Although she doubted he'd end up having a heart of gold and some magical cock that could make her orgasm on command.

She nearly laughed at that but bit her lip in time to stop it. She really didn't want to have to explain *why* she was laughing.

Magical cocks indeed.

Once she had her room assignment, another person came up to her and guided Tiffany down a hallway to show her where it was.

She took a quick peek over her shoulder, only to see David still staring.

Okay, it was getting a little weird now.

Maybe if she were lucky, she wouldn't have to deal with StoneRiver's clan leader again. It was hard to be nice, and charming, and fun for the children if he stared at her the whole time. Maybe he was afraid she'd fuck up? Or maybe he didn't trust humans?

Who knew?

But it didn't matter. No, the orphans were her top

priority for the next week. She was one of the activities instructors and would be outside most of the time anyway. She doubted David Lee would micromanage every single instructor for the week.

Taking a better hold on her duffel bag, she smiled at the person at her side and did her best to make small talk. Thankfully, the dragonwoman was friendly, and Tiffany soon forgot all about the broody clan leader and his stares.

Chapter Two

David had somehow managed to evade his cousin-in-law's questions about how he'd treated Tiffany Ford until the last volunteer checked in. As he moved to leave—the welcome reception for the volunteers would start soon—Megan took hold of his wrist and tugged. "This way."

Megan was mated to his cousin-slash-best-friend and was one of the few who didn't mind being blunt or direct with him. Oh, she knew not to challenge his dominance when it mattered, but as she shut the door to the small storage room and frowned up at him, he knew now wasn't one of those times. "What the hell was that about? Tiffany has been nothing but welcoming to the dragon-shifters, and I should know given how she works for my brother's mate at her bar and restaurant. Why the asshole moment back there?

And don't say it's nothing because I don't have time for lies."

His dragon laughed. *Yes, why was that again?*

Shut up.

Megan raised her eyebrows in question. "Well?"

Hell, he hadn't even told Justin—his cousin and Megan's mate—the truth. And yet, if he was going to try avoiding Tiffany as much as possible over the next week, he'd need help.

Megan was his second-in-command for the event and would very much be able to do that.

With a sigh, he decided what the hell. "I'll tell you, but first I need your promise to keep it a secret."

"Fine, whatever. As long as I can tell Justin, of course." He nodded his permission. "Then out with it."

"She's my true mate, Megan. Which means I need her to hate me."

Most people would laugh or say he was an idiot. But Megan knew his reasons even before he could explain them. "I know you and Justin both have this theory about the mates of StoneRiver clan leaders being doomed, but are you really ready to let her just slip through your fingers without even trying? You have me and Justin, but otherwise, you're lonely, David. Being a clan leader isn't easy, and a mate helps with it all."

He growled. "I know that. But I don't want to kill

her, Megan. Justin's mother was the last one to die. I thought you'd understand."

Justin's father had been clan leader before David. Even after his mate had been killed by some human bastards for sport, Jian Lee had done his best for StoneRiver up until right before he died.

And once David had won the clan leadership position, Jian had warned of ever repeating his mistake. Jian had thought he could beat the odds, but in the end, he hadn't been able to. He hadn't wanted David to go through the same kind of pain.

He didn't think himself superstitious, generally. However, five clan leader mates dying in a row was a fuck load of evidence to say he shouldn't dare risk anyone, let alone his true mate.

Megan finished searching his gaze and sighed. "I know it's not a trivial thing. But maybe try to at least be nice to her? Things have improved greatly over the last two decades when it comes to ADDA actually protecting dragon-shifters and arresting those who try to harm us. And since Tiffany isn't a dragon-shifter, she can't just fly away and accidentally get electrocuted in a lightning storm, either. None of those former clan leader mates who died were human. Maybe that's what StoneRiver needs to end the tragic cycle."

All five former mates had been dragon-shifters, true. For some reason, he'd been too focused on their deaths to think beyond that. "You and your logic."

Megan grinned. "Usually you love that about me."

He grumbled, "Yeah, whatever."

She raised her brows. "So you'll think about getting to know her a little before completely pushing her away? Brad knows her pretty well, and by all accounts, Tiffany isn't an idiot who'd rush into some kind of dangerous situation for the thrill of it."

Brad was Megan's brother and one of StoneRiver's Protectors, who was in charge of clan security. David trusted the male with his life. "I don't know."

"Think of it this way—as long as you don't kiss her, you're both safe." She lightly touched his arm. "Just think about it, okay? I hate seeing you so isolated and alone."

And with that, Megan left before he could reply.

So of course his dragon decided to speak up, not giving David a moment to think. *She's a very smart female.*

You only say that because it gets you closer to what you want.

Maybe. But she's right on two important points—the last time a clan leader's mate lived to old age, she was human. And second, Tiffany is safe unless we kiss her and claim her.

It seemed everyone was going to push him to be nice to the human, one way or the other.

He sighed. *I'm not making any grand decisions right this second. But I promise to at least be nice to her.*

That's hardly a change.

It'll have to be enough for now, dragon.

His beast huffed, but before he could reply, David exited the storage room and headed toward the large room being used to host the welcome reception.

No doubt Tiffany would be there. The only question was whether he'd risk talking with her or do his best to avoid her.

TIFFANY WALKED into the large room being used for the evening's reception and quickly scanned the crowd for any familiar faces.

She knew her boss, Tasha, wouldn't be there, nor her mate. At least for this evening. They were both working at Tasha's bar and restaurant.

Continuing her search, it seemed none of her brother's in-laws from PineRock had made it either. Which was strange, given how one cousin—Luna— had said she'd be here.

A male voice came from behind her. "If you tell me what kind of friend you're looking to make, I'll point you in the right direction."

She glanced over her shoulder to see a man with dark skin, black hair, and brown eyes. She'd seen him once or twice at the bar before, usually playing darts. She raised an eyebrow. "I didn't realize someone had the role of assigning friends for the week."

He grinned, and the man became too handsome for his own good. "It wasn't in the welcome packet, if that's what you mean." He moved to stand in front of her and put out a hand. "I'm Tyler Bell. And you're Tiffany Ford. I've seen you at the bar."

She shook his hand and nodded. "You like to play darts."

"No, I like to *win* at darts."

She couldn't help but smile. "Are there any dartboards around? I'm pretty good myself and like crushing the male ego every now and then."

He laughed. "You're going to make my night, aren't you?"

Used to men flirting with her at the bar, she decided not to encourage it. At least not right now.

She could tell from the tattoo peeking out from his shirt that he was a dragon-shifter, so she moved to safer territory. "Which clan are you from?"

"StoneRiver. My brother Jon is in charge of security, so if you need anything, ask me and I can reach him straight away."

Before she could ask if there was something she should be worried about, another male voice filled the air. "Tyler, your sister needs help with the sound system."

It was David Lee.

As Tiffany debated turning around to face his glare again, Tyler nodded. "I'll go." He looked back at Tiffany. "I'll see you around. If you ever need some advice about who to avoid, come find me."

She smiled again as Tyler raced off to a younger woman with the same shape of eyes and nose, who had to be his sister.

David moved to stand next to her. Even though he was at least a foot away, she was overly aware of his presence—strong, confident, and definitely broody.

She knew how to handle men like Tyler, those with easy charm and humor. But she had no fucking clue how to talk with David. Men like him tended to leave her alone at her job, and she was usually too swamped to try to crack any of them.

Thankfully he spoke again, saving her the trouble. "Come with me and I'll introduce you to some of the people you'll be working with."

She didn't think a clan leader had time to waste —after all, PineRock's leader was forever busy with paperwork and settling clan arguments. "If you introduce me to one, I should be fine after that. I'm sure there are tons of other things you need to do."

He finally met her gaze, his pupils flashing. "Everyone will be busy starting tomorrow. But tonight, it's my job to make sure you don't stand in a corner somewhere and feel abandoned."

She raised her brows. "I'm not a shy, hug-the-wall-and-hide-in-dark-corners type of woman. I just like to look around and observe before diving in."

His pupils flickered again. "Oh? And what have you noticed so far?"

Not caring that he was a clan leader in that moment, she pushed him gently to the side of the room, away from everyone else, and whispered as she nodded toward various people. "There's a guy over there who keeps trying to wink and smile at those three women. And whenever they can manage it without him seeing, they roll their eyes at one another. Clearly they're not interested in him." She gestured toward another group. "That group of young men are standing tall and keep interrupting each other. Either they're trying to outdo one another with stories or conquests or are about to start a fight." And she motioned toward one more group. "All of those people look a lot alike and easily touch each other without hesitation. I think they're related in some way." She finally looked back up at David and blinked at the surprise in his eyes. "Am I right?"

DAVID HAD NEVER MET SUCH a perceptive human before in his life.

Tiffany most definitely wasn't some stupid person who'd run headlong into danger without thought.

His dragon spoke up. *I'm glad you got jealous of Tyler and decided to talk with her.*

It wasn't jealousy.

Right, tell yourself that.

Okay, he had been a little jealous. Tyler was handsome and charming and closer to Tiffany's age. Not to mention unattached and free to go after any female he wanted without worrying if a kiss could end up threatening her life.

But seeing her with Tyler had made man and beast want to pull her close and growl to any male who came near her.

Which he had no right to do, of course.

Remembering Megan's words had finally made him cross the distance to Tiffany—*I hate seeing you so isolated and alone.*

The fact his cousin's mate was worried about him made David wonder if the clan as a whole did.

Which, in itself, could be a problem. Dragons needed a strong leader. And if they thought he was weak in any way, his control over the clan would start to crumble. Isolation was expected of leaders to a degree, but it was rare for one not to ever take a mate.

Not to mention inner dragons needed contact with others, to a degree. Otherwise, they could more easily turn rogue.

His dragon grunted. *I'm not weak.*

Of course you're not. But others may have opinions. And sometimes that is enough.

Then why fight your pull to this female? She could be good for us and *for the clan.*

I won't kiss her.

I didn't say you had to.

He didn't like how compliant his beast was being. Not at all.

So he'd decided to talk with her a little more, and then at least his clan members would see him talking with unknown females. That alone could help stave off the rumors for a while.

Which was why he was now standing next to the female and listening to Tiffany's observations. When she finished and asked, "Am I right?" he struggled with how to reply.

His beast said, *Just be truthful.*

David blurted, "You're good. But I'm curious, what do you see when you study me?"

She tilted her head and scrutinized him a second. "That's a hard one because usually I need to see people talking or interacting freely with others, with them not knowing I'm watching them. Right now, you could be trying to hide any number of things about yourself."

Despite everything, a smile tugged at his lips. "Does that mean you'll be spying on me this week to put together a report you'll hand in on the final day?"

She tapped her chin. "Hm, now there's an idea." She looked around to make sure no one was nearby and murmured, "What happens if you don't like what I find?"

He did finally smile. "Oh, I know what you'll find.

Maybe some require an ego-stroking, but I don't. A clan leader should know his faults because his enemies will also find them out."

She bit her bottom lip, and David's gaze instantly went to her pink lips. The bottom one was so full and inviting, making him want to replace his teeth with her own.

And standing this close to her, he couldn't help but notice the faint scent of pine and something entirely *her*.

Tiffany's words snapped his eyes back to hers. "In my experience, not many men want to hear the full truth."

He wanted to demand how she knew what males thought but wasn't about to give in to jealousy. Again.

No, David most definitely couldn't do that.

Instead, he shrugged. "An enemy will do their best to discover faults and exploit them, right? So it's better I accept them and plan what to do if someone tries to use them against my clan. Wes is the same way."

Wes Dalton was the leader of Clan PineRock, where Tiffany currently lived to be near her brother and his dragon-shifter mate.

Tiffany smiled. "He had one very big fault until Ashley made sure he realized it. Namely, he wanted her for *years* but was too afraid to make a move."

Since Ashley Swift had been the human ADDA employee overseeing his clan as well, until she'd mated Wes, he knew the story too. "He kept his distance to protect his clan. You're human, so you don't have to deal with ADDA like we do. It's a small miracle Wes was allowed to take Ashley as his mate, without facing any consequences."

She waved a hand in dismissal "Maybe once upon a time, but things have been changing, right? Otherwise Brad and Tasha wouldn't be together."

"Again, special circumstances. Tasha lives here for her safety."

The human female had been a target of the League. They'd destroyed her business back in Reno and had tried to "rescue" her from the dragon-shifters. Mating Brad had protected her, and they'd ended up blissfully besotted.

David pushed down the twinge of jealousy. He didn't have the same freedoms, after all. And he accepted that.

He had to.

Tiffany rolled her eyes. "Tell yourself it's only for Tasha's safety."

David resisted blinking. Was she such a good observer that she'd all but read his mind? "What do you mean by that?"

She shrugged. "Brad loves his mate and daughter more than anything. While safety is nice, Tasha lives here for Brad and their child since it's illegal for dragon-shifters to live in a human city." She leaned forward a fraction, and it took everything David had not to stare down the V of her neckline and get a glimpse of her small breasts. She added, "I think I've made my first observation about you, David. You either don't believe in, or are cynical about, love."

His dragon laughed, but David didn't give his beast a chance to say anything. Instead, he moved a fraction closer to Tiffany, ignoring how her cheeks heated at his close proximity. "Love exists, I see it all the time. But while some people can fall in love and live a carefree life, we don't all have that luxury."

She searched his gaze. "There's no law saying a clan leader can't have a mate and love them."

This close David could see her hazel eyes were more brown than green. "Maybe not a law, but it's fucking dangerous for some."

Her brows came together. "What are you talking about?"

His first instinct was to smooth away the lines of her face, make her smile again, and tell her she never needed to worry. He'd take care of her.

And that made him take a few steps backward, reason returning to his brain the more distance he put between them.

Because he wouldn't be able to take care of her. Eventually she'd be hurt because of him.

It'd been selfish talking to her tonight. He'd need to correct that going forward.

His dragon growled. *Don't push her away.*

Ignoring his beast, David cleared his throat.

"You're determined to observe me, right? Then I won't give away all the answers. If you're as good as you say, find out the answer yourself."

Without another word, David walked away and did his best to calm his thundering heartbeat.

He'd been too close to her, loving how she treated him as a male instead of a leader and had wanted nothing more than to tell her anything and everything she wanted.

Which was fucking ridiculous.

Of course now he'd laid down a challenge, one he simultaneously wanted her to meet and to fail.

His dragon laughed. *You aren't going to last a week near her.*

Shut up, dragon. After tonight, we'll be too busy to notice the human.

Tell yourself that. His dragon paused a second before whispering, *This is going to be fun.*

A small part of David longed for a little bit of fun, something he hadn't had in over a decade.

Too many things had happened over the years with changing regulations, inter-clan disputes, and even the rise in anti-dragon extremists that David hadn't thought much about it beyond doing his duty to deal with it all.

And yet, imagining Tiffany teasing him before daring him to chase her stirred his blood.

After one conversation with Tiffany Ford, he was in a fucking lot of trouble. The only question was if he could be strong enough to resist her, especially if she made any sort of attempt to better get to know him.

Pushing aside the doubt, he worked on rebuilding the calm, strong facade he usually wore. Once he managed that, he went about greeting guests and ensuring the final details were all set for the next day.

David managed to avoid looking at Tiffany for the rest of the evening. Only when he was set to retire did he steal a glance at her, over in the corner talking to Tyler and his sister.

And she stared right at him.

Ignoring the shot of awareness at her gaze, he turned and exited the room.

It was going to be a long fucking week. And he had no one to blame but himself.

Chapter Three

The next day, Tiffany watched the twenty-odd children run through the obstacle course she and a dragonman named Seth had set up and smiled at how they laughed as they tried to outdo each other.

Once upon a time, she'd wanted to be an elementary school teacher. However, even though she now knew she had dyslexia, no one had figured it out until she was well into her teens. As a result, she'd grown frustrated with reading and had decided not to voluntarily go through more schooling after high school.

True, one teacher had helped her tremendously in her sophomore year of high school, to the point Tiffany mostly could handle reading for short periods without too much trouble, but the damage had been done.

Although, because she'd struggled with reading for so long, she'd instead learned to watch people. Faces, mannerisms, even little signs of nervousness. While she couldn't always tell when someone was lying, she had gotten better at judging the truth versus lies over the years.

Dragon-shifters were harder to gauge, though working at both the bar and as a server in Tasha's place had given her lots of practice watching them, and she was slowly learning how to read the two personalities in one body.

Which she was going to need to give David his silly report.

She could've said no, of course. But the interaction the night before was different than when he'd first greeted her, and it had intrigued her.

Yes, that was the reason. Not because he'd stared at her lips and made her heart race, in a good way.

Stop it, Tiff. She didn't want to get silly over a man, not even a dragonman.

Maybe if she ended up someone's true mate, she'd think about it. But her family's past, with her one brother stealing the wife of his twin, made her doubt her instincts about men at times. It had worked out for Ryan in the end with his dragonwoman, but up until the wife-stealing debacle, Tiffany had adored her other older brother, Mark, as well. The fact he'd hurt Ryan without even saying anything and then ran away, severing all contact with her too, still made her heart heavy.

But as the children came ever closer toward her and the dragonman helping her, where the finish line was, Tiffany pushed aside her family history to smile and cheer them on.

A brown-haired little girl raced across the line first and did a little dance, her pupils flashing from round to slits and back again at the same time. Her name tag said, "Madison, age 10," and Tiffany put up a hand for a high five. "Awesome job, Madison!"

Madison slapped her hand against Tiffany's as she grinned. "Thanks, Miss Tiffany. Can we do it again? I think I can do it even faster next time."

She grinned back at the girl's enthusiasm. "But if we do this course again, you'll miss out on the next challenge."

The girl's eyes widened. "There's another one?"

A little boy asked, "What is it? Maybe I can beat Maddy at it."

Madison stuck out her tongue. "I doubt it. You're too slow, Landon."

Tiffany laughed. "It's only the first day. Trust me, there are tons of things to do over the entire week. But just know having fun is the most important part. Winning is just a bonus."

A familiar male voice said from behind her, "You haven't hung around dragon-shifter children very often, have you?"

She whirled to face David, trying not to frown at him sneaking up on her. Why did he keep doing that? "I can't say I have. But still, having fun is important too."

"For humans, you can easily say that. However, the inner dragons of most of these little ones only just started talking to them in the last couple of years. And trust me, our inner beasts can be quite demanding in the beginning."

She raised her eyebrows. "I thought they were rather demanding all the time, according to my sister-in-law."

David chuckled, the action making his face relaxed. Not only did he look younger, but he also became altogether too handsome.

Of course, she shouldn't notice such things. He was clan leader, stoic most of the time, and most definitely not interested in her. He merely wanted to ensure the event ran well. Yes, that was all.

And she wouldn't let that bother her.

He replied, "Yes, that's true. Dragons are demanding about certain things." His pupils flashed, and she wondered what his inner beast had said. Before she could even think of asking, he continued, "Although every dragon-shifter has to learn how to control them, to a degree, from a young age. Otherwise they can turn rogue."

And even she had learned that rogue dragons

could be executed by ADDA, if they felt the dragon in question was a threat.

Not wanting to focus on the grim side of his statement, she decided to keep it light. Tapping her chin, Tiffany replied, "Well, the human half stays in control except during mate-claim frenzies, as Gabby tells me. Because trying to control an inner dragon during a frenzy is fairly impossible, right?"

David froze and Tiffany resisted a frown. Truth be told, she didn't know if David had had a true mate before and lost her, which could explain his reaction. All she knew was what Wes had told her before leaving for the event—that David was single.

Why he'd done that, she didn't know. It'd been an odd revelation. However, she knew Wes wasn't conniving enough to try and push one of his clan toward the leader, all for the sake of an alliance, either.

Since David still hadn't said a word, she raised her brows. "Afraid to admit I'm right about frenzies? I didn't think you'd give up so easily."

His pupils flashed a few times, but his face relaxed, and he shrugged. "You're right. But frenzies are meant to be enjoyed, not feared. Indulging dragons from an early age can lead to problems later on. And the last thing you want is a rogue dragon, the human half unable to wrestle control, meaning ADDA will find them and shoot them down."

Yes, it was true and such incidents sometimes

even made the news. But it wasn't something she wanted to discuss in front of a group of young children.

Besides, as the children finished their juice and snacks, she knew she needed to focus on them again.

Although, for some reason, she wished she could talk more with David about it all, beyond the whisperings in the news and the rumors. Many people on PineRock still tiptoed around her. They'd tell her all about frenzies and what their dragons said but tended to avoid more serious topics like the League and ADDA in general.

So far, David had talked about anything she'd brought up without brushing it aside.

Which was rather nice, for a change.

Seth signaled that they needed to go to the next area, so she pushed aside the desire to chat longer with David and said, "I need to help my partner get the children ready for the next activity. So unless there's something important you need to tell me, I should go."

"No, there's nothing. Go on and help Seth."

She studied him a beat before turning back toward the children. And even though she didn't see David for the rest of the day, she swore she felt his eyes on her.

Stop being paranoid. Wes trusted David and had said as much.

It was just her mind being weird. And so Tiffany

did her best to forget about the clan leader and focused on giving the children the most fun she could. Especially since the next day would be a little more stressful, given how some prospective parents were coming to meet them.

Chapter Four

The following evening, David straightened his tie and jacket before he entered the large room where prospective parents and the orphan children would meet.

Dragon-shifters hated formal attire, and David was no different. But ADDA helped with any adoptions, and so when it came to these types of events, they required everyone to be dressed formally.

As if dressing well would make everything perfect, or some shit like that.

His dragon snorted. *They like their rules.*

And yet, the rules are going to make every single person in this room uncomfortable, most of all the children. How can they be themselves if they're constricted in fancy clothes?

I agree, but there's not much we can do about it.

Since his inner beast was right, David mentally

grunted and went over to the table where Megan and a few others would sign people in.

He'd just opened his mouth to ask if everything was ready when Tiffany Ford walked into the room.

She wore a simple black dress that hugged the upper part of her body before flaring at her hips and ending right above her knees. Her hair was swept up atop her head, in a sort of messy bun, which only highlighted her beautiful eyes and graceful neck.

Even without any lace, or ribbons, or whatever adorned dresses these days, she was the most beautiful female he'd ever seen.

Oh, she was always pretty. But tonight, she seemed to almost glow.

And he wondered why.

His cousin-in-law poked his arm with a pen. She murmured, "You'll catch flies like that."

David promptly shut his mouth and forced himself to look away from Tiffany. He asked Megan, "Is everything ready?"

His cousin-in-law raised her brows, but no doubt aware of the others nearby, she let the matter drop. For now. "Yes, everything's ready. So stop worrying. Justin is handling the backend of things, so just do your part, mingle, and try to be a little charming. If you can manage it, of course."

Megan's teasing tone made him want to do something childish, like stick out his tongue. Instead, he grunted and murmured, "I'll start now."

His dragon laughed. *None of the children or guests have arrived yet.*

Ignoring his beast, he couldn't help but walk up to Tiffany. She stopped arranging the cookies on a plate to look up at him.

For a second, they merely stared at each other, time stilling, almost as if there was no one else in the room.

After seeing her with the children the day before, as well as her yet again treating him as a male and not a leader, he'd dreamed about kissing her, claiming her, making her scream his name as she came around his cock.

All the things he could never have but couldn't seem to stop dreaming about.

Tiffany was the first to speak. "You clean up nice."

He barely resisted tugging at his tie and ripping the damn thing off. "You look like a fairy-tale princess."

As soon as the words came out, he wanted to groan. David wasn't the most charming of males, and yet he'd wanted to say something more than how pretty she was.

The corner of Tiffany's mouth ticked up before she brushed her skirts and then pointed toward her feet. "I'm smarter than a princess, though. I won't lose a shoe or struggle to run away, if some villain comes around."

He noticed her black and white shoes, a sort of nicer-looking sneaker. Smiling, he met her eyes again. "Nothing wrong with a practical princess."

"Hm, but I think I'd rather be the queen. Then I'd be in charge."

His dragon hummed. *She could be* our *queen.*

He focused on Tiffany and not his dragon. "Of course. I couldn't imagine you as a princess, sitting around, eating chocolate and waiting for someone to rescue you."

She snorted. "Definitely not. Better than a queen, I was the knight not too long ago. I helped my brother find his dragon mate, after all."

Before he could think better of it, he blurted, "But what about you?"

She blinked. "Excuse me?"

"I mean, are you looking for yours now too? A dragon mate?"

Before she could answer, the doors opened, and the children were brought in first. Tiffany finished laying out the last cookies before she smiled. "I need to go help wrangle them."

He nodded, and she left, not so much walking as striding toward her charges, ready to keep them in line for what was sure to be a long two hours for all involved.

Although he wondered if part of her haste was to get as far away from him as she could, to avoid answering his question.

Which he still couldn't believe he'd asked.

His dragon spoke up. *I think you asked because you wanted to know the answer.*

It doesn't matter what she says, dragon. She's not meant to be ours.

Bullshit, and you know it. But I don't think you'll last the week, so I'm not too worried.

He resisted a frown. *I'm merely being nice to her, as I should.*

Right, tell yourself that.

As he tried to think of a way to win the argument, Jon Bell, his head Protector in charge of security, came up and said it was time to let the adults in.

So as he and Jon discussed a few last-minute details, David quickly forgot about his blunder. More than one child's life could be changed this evening, and he needed to do everything he could to help some of them find new homes.

Which meant talking to the guests and doing his best to see if any of them set off warning bells. True, ADDA and the orphanage had screened them, but David knew what people said in an interview or on paper didn't always match them in real life.

He would be an extra layer of protection, and that meant forgetting about Tiffany and her beautiful hazel eyes.

Well, at least for the next two hours. He wasn't so sure he could forget her completely.

Tiffany was kept so busy getting children to the right areas—little tables set up around the edges of the room, with clear plastic barriers acting as walls for a small amount of privacy—that she barely had a moment to think of anything else.

But as she double-checked that her last charge, Madison, sat talking with the couple across from her, Tiffany had nothing else to do but walk around and occasionally check on the kids.

Which meant her mind finally had a chance to wander back to her conversation with David and what he'd asked her: *"I mean, are you looking for yours now too? A dragon mate?"*

Why would he ask her that? Surely he wasn't trying to see if she wanted him as one.

Or was he?

She had no fucking clue.

But as she watched him exit one little partitioned area and enter another to chat with the prospective parents and the child across from them, she decided to ignore his weird question and instead focus on watching him to better research for her report.

Nibbling a cookie, she watched as he sat at the open side of the table, with the couple on one side and the child on the other, and did his best to chat with them all.

Over the last day, Tiffany had discovered the six-year-old boy to David's side was one of the shyer ones. Even now he kept swinging his feet and looking at the table. David said something, the boy's head jerked up. One of the prospective fathers—the two dragonmen were hoping to finally have a child of their own—asked a question, and the little dragon boy started chatting away.

Soon the two males and the boy were smiling and laughing, and not long after, David exited the makeshift room to head to the next.

Even though the dragon leader seemed to be hot and cold with her, not to mention somewhat intense at times, Tiffany started to understand why he'd been clan leader for a decade or so. David was good at getting people to talk to one another, even if he said little himself.

No doubt that helped with settling clan disputes or working with the American Department of Dragon Affairs.

But she still wondered what he was like without the eyes of the clan on him. Did he relax? Ever do something simply because he wanted to and not because it would help his people?

Even if she watched him the entire week, Tiffany wasn't entirely sure she'd find that out unless she cornered him at his house or something.

Which she most assuredly shouldn't—no, wouldn't—do.

Something caught her eye on the far side of the

room, distracting her thoughts. She noticed little Madison sitting across from a man and woman, inching her chair back until it hit the plastic barrier. It didn't wobble—they had been secured to prevent that—but she could see Madison trying to move even farther away.

Something was wrong.

Without thinking, she went over and popped her head in, plastering a fake smile on her face. "How's everyone doing with drinks? Do I need to get you guys anything else?"

She chanced a glance at Madison, and at the fear in the little girl's eyes, Tiffany's instinct was confirmed —something had happened. The feeling increased when the woman said coolly, "No, we have plenty, thank you. Now, if you'll excuse us, we're trying to get to know little Madison here."

Madison reached out and grabbed Tiffany's hand. Even without saying a word, she knew the little girl didn't want to be left alone with the pair.

A quick glance told Tiffany that the man had a glint in his eyes as he stared at the little dragon girl, as if he were awaiting a special treat.

It made Tiffany's skin crawl.

And the woman looked adoringly at her husband, as if she'd do anything for him. She'd bet everything she owned that whatever the man was up to, the woman was part of it.

The sick feeling in the pit of Tiffany's stomach

told her that whatever screenings had been done, they'd failed. Maybe the pair had been able to hide their true intent when talking only with the adults. But apparently, the sick bastard couldn't do so in the presence of the little girl.

Just as Tiffany was trying to figure out a way to get Madison out without causing a scene, David appeared at her side. He briefly met her gaze, his pupils flashed to slits and back, and Tiffany tried to tell him without words about the uneasiness in her gut.

She had no idea if it worked or not. But in the next beat, David said smoothly, "I think it's time for your interview with me, Mr. and Mrs. Dunn. Miss Ford, can you take Maddy to the activity room so I can have a private word?"

There was no activity room set up for the night, nor did she think there were any sort of individual interviews.

But Tiffany wasn't stupid. David had either understood her silent message or had realized the same thing she had about the man.

She nodded and gently pulled Madison up and slightly behind her. "Come on, Maddy."

The couple protested, but Tiffany left without another glance, tugging Madison out of the main room and into a small room used for some of the week's craft activities.

Once inside, the little girl hugged her. "Thank you for not leaving me behind, Miss Tiffany."

She stroked the girl's hair to soothe her. Carefully, she asked, "What had you so scared, Maddy?" When the girl said nothing, she knelt down until she was eye level. "Tell me, Madison. It's okay."

Madison's pupils flashed between slits and round a few times before she blurted, "They s-said not to, or I'd never get adopted."

The tears in the little girl's eyes broke Tiffany's heart. According to her file, the little girl had been abandoned by some human mother who'd been involved with a dragonman, with not even a note about her true parents. No doubt Madison had dreamed of being adopted and having a family for years and years.

Something else the manipulative couple no doubt knew and played upon.

Despite her internal rolling anger, Tiffany somehow kept her voice firm yet gentle. "That's a lie, Maddy. You're special, and you'll find the right family. I know you will." She tucked a section of hair behind Madison's ears. "Now, tell me what happened. I promise you won't get into trouble."

With a lot of coaxing and pausing for Madison to catch her breath, Tiffany put it all together.

The man had asked if she liked sharing her bath because he'd very much like to help her wash. When she'd said she was too old for that, the woman had said no, of course not. And it wasn't right to tell any father no. She should be grateful and do whatever the man asked of her.

Including sharing her bed sometimes, to hug close and cuddle.

Tiffany knew it wasn't for any sort of fucking cuddling.

And if she saw the bastard again, she'd kick his ass using all the self-defense training she'd learned from the dragon-shifters over the months since she'd moved to PineRock.

After convincing Madison that she'd been right to be afraid and that she'd talk to Mr. Lee and the others, the girl had calmed down. Tiffany had managed to get Madison to do some coloring as they waited. Eventually, David and his cousin-in-law Megan walked in.

From the fury in David's eyes, he'd most likely found out—or at least sensed—what had happened.

Megan was the one to squat down next to Madison and say, "If it's okay, would you like to come spend the night at my house? I have three little boys that are sort of a handful but love to play with others, even females. You'll have your own bed, and I'm sure even the cat will want to snuggle with you. What do you say?"

Madison looked at Tiffany, and she nodded in encouragement. "You should go. Miss Megan's really nice, and I'd go just to see the cat. Word is that he's really fluffy."

Megan smiled and nodded. "He is that. If you pet his belly, he'll love you forever."

Madison bit her lip and said, "I love kitties. What's his name?"

Megan replied, "It's Mischief. I know it's weird, but it suits him. So what do you say, do you want to come meet him? And maybe we'll even have pancakes tomorrow morning for breakfast, if you like."

"Chocolate chip pancakes?" Madison asked shyly.

With a huge smile, the dragonwoman said, "What other kind are there?" She put out her hand. "So what do you say, Madison?"

The little dragon girl eventually placed her small hand in Megan's. However, Madison looked at Tiffany and asked, "I'll see you tomorrow, Miss Tiffany, right?"

She smiled. "Of course. We still have that relay race to do, and I'm curious to see if you can beat Landon again."

Her pupils flashed. "I'll win. You'll see."

Megan gently asked Madison about her races and eventually got her out the door. Once they were alone, Tiffany murmured, "Thanks for understanding and helping back there."

As David's pupils flashed rapidly, she couldn't fully judge his mood. However, she held her ground.

While she didn't think he was angry at her, she had somewhat overstepped her authority.

And she'd do it again, if need be, to protect a child.

Standing tall, she waited to see what he'd say.

David was beyond furious.

At ADDA, at the failure of multiple screenings, and even himself for not noticing the fucking pervert earlier.

On top of that, Tiffany had dealt with the bastard and his simpering wife on her own.

Even if he didn't think they would've done anything to Tiffany in a room full of people, she'd been so close to danger. After talking with the pair, it wouldn't surprise him if the deranged wife would've killed Tiffany if it meant pleasing her husband.

His dragon spoke up. *She's fine and did well. Why can't you see that part?*

Because it just shows that even talking with me stirs up trouble. She most definitely needs to stay away from me.

Don't be fucking stupid. This has nothing to do with the past or the tragedies.

Maybe later, when he wasn't angry, he'd realize that.

But at the moment, staring at Tiffany as she stood tall and lifted her chin a fraction, all he could think of was the couple hurting her. Maybe even killing her.

And at that thought, his heart hurt. He nearly put his hand over it to try and soothe the pain.

His dragon growled. *Just stop with the self-flagellation and talk with her already. She looks like we're about to scold her, which is the farthest thing from the truth. At least let her know she's not in trouble.*

At his beast's words, his anger faded a fraction. He wanted to protect her, not scare her. He cleared his throat and said, "It's me that should be thanking you. It seems your observation skills saved a little girl tonight."

She blinked, and her posture relaxed a fraction before she waved a hand in dismissal. "I don't need thanks. Just tell me that asshole is being reported as we speak."

He nodded. "Jon is locking the couple up and calling ADDA. Since the couple is from a clan in Utah, I have no authority over them. If I did, it wouldn't be pretty."

She nodded. "I'm only sorry I can't kick his ass and show him what someone his own size can do to him."

With the fire blazing in her eyes, he couldn't help but admire her. Even though she was human and at a big disadvantage against a pair of dragon-shifters, she didn't blink at trying to take them on.

She most definitely wasn't some defenseless princess waiting to be rescued.

Needing some sort of levity to help control his desire to kill the fucker currently locked away, he said, "I was wrong to call you a princess, or even a queen. You're definitely the knight, ready to take on anything to protect those who need it."

Some of the tension left her body, and she almost smiled. "I still say I'm a queen, but one who can also kick ass. And in the fantasy, maybe even learn to use a sword or dagger."

David did smile at the image of her jumping up from a throne to punch some bastard in the throat before kicking him in the balls.

All while wearing a tight leather outfit, blades sheathed at her waist, and her long hair secured up with the comb his great-grandmother had brought with her from China.

He resisted a frown. No, not the comb. It was only something he'd give his mate, and Tiffany wasn't that.

His dragon said, *She could be. Tiffany seems like she could handle anything. Who knows what Wes has taught her. We could teach her additional techniques so she'd be able to defend herself even more.*

The thought of Wes Dalton standing behind Tiffany, correcting her stance, caused a thread of jealousy to dance through him.

Which was fucking stupid. Wes had his own mate,

a female who'd probably fight anyone who tried to take her mate from her.

Focusing back on his beast's words, David thought his dragon believed Tiffany could face whatever trouble StoneRiver faced.

David was beginning to wonder the same thing.

However, he wasn't going to dwell on that right now. Both he and Tiffany needed to go back out to the main room and try their best to finish their jobs for the night. Despite what had happened with Madison, David knew it was an anomaly. Most of the couples were genuinely looking for a child to raise and love. Both man and beast had sensed how most of the adults and children yearned to find one another, to have a family.

Something David didn't think he'd ever have but was starting to think could be possible.

His dragon muttered, *About fucking time.*

Ignoring his beast, he put out his arm. "We should get back to the others. And maybe before I go finish my interviews, you can tell me what else you've noticed? If there's anything off, anything at all, I want you to tell me."

If she was surprised at his sudden change of topic, she didn't show it. "I don't think anyone else gives off the same creepy vibe. A few of the couples don't suit, I think. But not because they're perverted fuckers."

His lips twitched at her choice of words—her

straightforward manner was somewhat endearing—
and moved his offered arm once more in invitation.
"Then tell me as we walk. Once we get back to the
main room, we'll move extra slowly, just to make sure
you have time to tell me everything."

After a beat, she threaded her arm through his
and nodded. "Okay."

At the heat of her arm against his, David wanted
to pull her close and feel more of her softer body
against him.

Much more.

But he pushed aside the thought and instead
focused on Tiffany's observations. This evening was
about the children.

Although come morning, David wasn't so sure he
could keep his distance from the human female.

Which might be a problem, as his resolve to resist
her weakened by the minute.

Chapter Five

The following day, Tiffany somehow managed to keep the kids entertained and hide just how tired she was.

She hadn't slept, and not entirely because of the close call with Madison. The dragon girl was staying with Megan and her mate, and Tiffany didn't like to dwell on what-ifs for the past. Madison was safe; that was all that mattered.

No, the sleepless night was because of David.

He'd listened to everything she'd said with interest, asked clarifying questions, and shared his own observations as well. In a strange way, helping Madison had almost made them…a team.

And while that was strange to think about, it was when he'd wished her goodnight that had kept her up.

They'd been alone in a corridor. He'd gazed

down at her, and she could've sworn heat had flashed in his eyes.

But the intensity had been gone before she could blink, and he'd stepped back and returned to his damn formality, bidding her goodnight. As some of her fellow volunteers ushered her along, she'd lost yet another chance to ask him about his weird looking-for-a-dragon-mate question.

All through the night, she'd wondered if his question had a point. Namely, was she his true mate?

But she'd finally decided she couldn't be. A dragon-shifter finding their true mate was supposed to be a blessing, or so she'd been told. One most couldn't wait to find and share the news.

Mostly because a kiss with a true mate would start off a mate-claim frenzy, one that would only stop when the woman was pregnant. And warning the partner was usually a good idea, to avoid any sort of mistaken kisses.

David seemed super responsible, to the point he'd probably have warned her right away.

And she wasn't sure how she felt about the true mate option being off the table. She'd never been good with men romantically, and at least with true mates, it usually meant the dragon's best chance at happiness.

Those were odds that Tiffany wanted, if she were to try with anyone.

Of course it was entirely possible she wasn't any

dragon-shifter's true mate. Just because she secretly wanted it didn't mean it'd happen.

As she cleaned up the last of the equipment for the day, she was just about to go to her room to freshen up before dinner when Megan Lee walked toward her.

Smiling, Tiffany waved and went to meet the taller dragonwoman. Megan spoke first. "I'm glad I caught you. Do you want to come over to dinner at my house? Maddy is going to stay with us for the whole week, and she's been bugging me and Justin to invite you over too."

She searched Megan's gaze. "So she's doing okay then?"

The dragonwoman nodded. "I think between my six-year-old son, Andy, and the cat, she's forgotten about most everything else. It seems Maddy likes playing the role of older sister." She lowered her voice. "And it's been kind of nice. Not that I leave her in charge or anything, but Andy seems to listen to her. I think it's because her dragon talks with her, and his still hasn't spoken to him yet. And so he keeps asking questions on how to get his beast to talk with him."

Her brows came together. "Is that how it works? You have to coax them out?"

Megan looked at her funny a second before asking slowly, "Didn't Wes and the others give you some books on dragon-shifter basics?"

They had, but reading wasn't high on her list of fun activities. And apparently, dragon-shifters didn't make audio versions, either, which was how she usually enjoyed books. "Er, yes. But I've been super busy helping Gaby and Ryan with their baby, as well as working for Tasha. I'm usually too tired to read at night."

Megan shrugged. "Well, the inner dragon is silent for the first six or seven years, hiding in a partition in the mind. Once it does finally emerge and speak, that's when the trouble starts since the kid has to learn to control the second personality inside their head. Usually in the beginning, the dragon half tries to dominate the human one."

"Interesting," she murmured. "But how does the sheltered dragon end up with a stronger personality, I wonder. Because they're wild or something?"

Megan smiled. "I think you definitely need some mini-lessons, Tiff. So that decides it—you're coming to dinner, and I won't take no for an answer. Between me, Justin, the children, and David, you'll have a fount of knowledge at your disposal."

She tried to sound casual as she asked, "David will be there?"

Megan studied her a beat. "He's my husband's cousin—although, truth be told, I'd call them more brothers than cousins—and he often comes over. David couldn't cook if his life depended on it, and I won't have him starve."

She smiled at the image of Megan fussing over David, forcing him to eat. "I had to do something similar for my brother, after his wife left him."

As soon as the words were out, she mentally kicked herself. She didn't talk about that period of time with anyone. Mostly because Ryan had been a hot mess, and she didn't want to violate his privacy.

Megan gave her a look of understanding, one that told of some kind of story, as she said, "We do what we must to help our brothers, don't we?" She gestured toward the outdoor activity area. "Is everything cleaned up or do you need some help?"

"No, I'm done. I just hope I have enough time to shower and change before dinner."

"Of course." Megan gave her the directions and added, "I'll let Jon and the others know you're coming to my house. So don't worry about getting through security. I'll see you soon."

Tiffany raced back to her room to clean up. It was a treat to be invited onto a dragon clan's land, and she wasn't going to miss the opportunity. All the volunteers were staying just outside the gated main area of StoneRiver and weren't supposed to go into StoneRiver proper until the final night, with a sendoff party.

Although as she hurried to get ready, it was more than seeing StoneRiver that made her heart pound. She would not only get answers to some of the questions she always forgot to ask her brother's mate, but she'd also get to see David.

Part of her wanted him to be cool and distant again, so she'd stop thinking about him.

And yet, the other half wanted him to treat her like the night before, as an equal and confidante.

Well, and she wouldn't mind a few heated glances, either, to let her know if she was being a fool about the dragon leader or not.

But she wouldn't know any of that until she arrived. So after one last glance in the mirror, she walked as quickly as possible toward StoneRiver's main gates.

DAVID WAS LOSING—BADLY—AT some sort of children's game against his six-year-old honorary nephew and ten-year-old Madison when Megan came into the room, Tiffany right behind her.

He should've stood to greet them, but all he could do was stare at the human female.

Tiffany had a tight-fitting black tank top, blue jeans, and black boots on, with her long hair streaming down her back. The clothes were simple, and yet they hugged every curve of her body, from her lovely round hips—and he knew from her activity clothes, a perfect plump ass—to her small breasts.

He'd seen her dressed like this once before,

months ago at an event at Tasha's bar and restaurant, but he'd somehow forced himself to forget about it.

His dragon spoke up. *I never did. Imagine fucking her with nothing but her boots on.*

David did his best not to picture it, but failed.

Tiffany sitting on the desk in his office, her thighs splayed wide as she lightly caressed her wet pussy, waiting for him to come claim her.

Wearing nothing but a pair of high, black boots and a small tattoo on her hip.

As if he'd know if she had a tattoo or not.

He had to take a second to keep his cock soft.

Madison poked his arm. "Are you okay, Mr. David?"

Closing his mouth and remembering he was in the presence of children, he tamed his libido, stood, and said, "I'm fine. I was just remembering something."

Megan rolled her eyes, but he ignored her to walk up to Tiffany. "I didn't know you'd be here tonight."

She raised an eyebrow. "Megan invited me, so I came."

His beast snorted. *I'd like to make her come a few times with nothing more than our tongue.*

Ignoring his beast, he cleared his throat. Since charming her would be a disaster, he asked, "What do you think of StoneRiver?"

From the corner of his eye, he noticed Megan sigh and look upward. No doubt she wished he was more like her mate, Justin, who had smiles and laughter for just about everyone, without even trying.

Tiffany smiled. "It seems nice, not much different from PineRock, if I'm honest—lots of hills, mountains, and houses. Although I did notice a giant climbing wall on the way in, which we don't have."

He asked quickly, "Do you like to climb?"

She shrugged, and he most definitely didn't notice her breasts bounce. Nope, he didn't.

His dragon merely laughed.

She replied, "Not mountains and the like, but the wall looks like fun. If you couldn't tell from the job I volunteered for, I like to be active."

His dragon purred, *That could be arranged.*

Before he could stop himself, he blurted, "Then maybe we should try the wall and have a race to the top."

She raised her brows. "But you've probably done it a million times, so that wouldn't be fair."

He shook his head. "I haven't climbed it since I was a boy. And I could give you a head start, to even the playing field."

She stared at him like he was a little crazy. Not that he could blame her. Who suddenly blurted a challenge to climb a rock wall?

But even though he shouldn't care, he wanted to impress her with something besides settling clan disputes or some other bureaucratic bullshit.

Not to mention seeing her flushed cheeks

afterward would definitely be a bonus. As would be watching her ass as she took her head start.

Madison said, "I'd love to watch that! You'd be so awesome, Miss Tiffany. I bet you could beat Mr. David, even if he's a dragon and you're not."

Her gaze finally went to the dragon girl. "Hm, it would be cool to win against him, wouldn't it?" She met his gaze again, amusement dancing in her eyes. "Especially if there's a wager."

His dragon snorted. *I like that idea too. Our boon could be licking her pussy with our tongue.*

Megan jumped in. "Dinner won't be for an hour or so, and I have some clothes Tiffany could wear. You two could go, and I'll hold down the fort here with the children."

Madison said, "But Miss Megan, I want to see them race!"

Andy, Megan's son, said, "Me too, Mom."

Megan shook her head. "No, I think it's better for them to go alone this time. I don't want you two getting any ideas." She fixed her gaze on David, her pupils flashing, before asking, "So, what will it be?" She shifted her eyes to the human. "Should I go get some clothes for you to change into, Tiffany?"

As he stared into Tiffany's eyes, he held his breath.

He wanted her to say yes. Even if his cousin was trying to set them up, trying to convince him to give the female a chance, he didn't care.

David hadn't done anything fun for a long, long time, and now he could think of nothing else but him racing against Tiffany, maybe even taunting her on purpose, to try and get to the top of the wall first.

Even if this was the only memory he could make with her with the two of them alone and having fun, he'd take it.

She finally grinned. "I say let's do it. And we can discuss the wager on the way."

His dragon grunted. *Good. Now, I have a few ideas for the wager…*

As his beast listed a number of things—all of them involving her naked—David ignored him.

He needed to concentrate if he wanted to win, which meant keeping a cool head and his cock soft.

TIFFANY COULD FEEL David's eyes on her as she walked out the front door of Megan's house, dressed in a sports bra and shorts that were a little too small.

She and Megan wore the same shoe size and sports bra. However, Megan's butt was smaller by quite a bit.

Thank goodness for the stretchy material.

Because ever since she'd said yes to the rock climb challenge, she wanted nothing else but to do it and win against David.

The dragonman in question fell in step beside her

and asked, "Tell me the truth—have you done one of these walls before?"

She nodded. "I worked for a time at a rec center, one with a wall, in my late teens. It may have been a few years since the last time I tried climbing, but I think it's like riding a bicycle, and you never forget." Although in the haste to change and get going, she'd forgotten to ask one very important point. "Are there harnesses and safety gear? I can't exactly extend wings from my back and glide down."

The corners of his mouth twitched up. "That's not exactly how it works."

"Well, even if it doesn't, dragon-shifters have superhero-like reflexes, and I don't."

He nodded. "We don't usually have the safety gear for the reasons you mentioned, unless minors are on the wall, but I already texted Maya, one of the Protectors and safety instructors for the wall, to meet us. She'll be in charge of your harness and safety."

She frowned up at him. "What about you?"

He shrugged. "I won't fall."

"But you could."

His pupils flashed a beat before he replied, "Don't worry about me, Tiffany. I'll be fine."

She'd never been good at small talk or beating around the bush, so she blurted, "But if you fell, and you can't just extend your wings, you could still get hurt or die if you hit your head on the way down. Reflexes won't help you then."

"We'll only be racing to the first ledge, and I have fast reflexes. It'll be fine."

For a beat, Tiffany wondered if anyone ever worried about David himself. He was clan leader, and it was his job to look after the entire clan.

But who looked after him?

Oh, she thought his cousin and his mate probably did. But even they had a busy household with three children and probably didn't know half of what David put himself through.

Although why it mattered so much to her, she didn't know.

She bit her lip before sighing. "Fine, I'll take you at your word. But just know that if you fall and hurt yourself, and it's only a minor injury, I'm not going to take the high road."

"And if I do get hurt? Which I won't, by the way."

She raised her brows. "Then I'm going to make sure you get better so I can whoop your ass myself."

His lips twitched as his pupils flashed. "That would be quite the sight."

She looked at him askance. "Why do I think you want me to try and do exactly that?"

Heat flashed in his eyes a beat before he cleared his throat. "There are many things I want but can't have."

His question piqued her curiosity. "What the hell are you talking about?"

He opened his mouth to reply, but a dragonwoman spotted them and waved. David returned the gesture. "That's Maya. The wall's just ahead." He took her hand and lightly tugged. "Come on."

For a few beats, all she could do was revel in the hot, slightly rough feel of his hand in hers. The way it engulfed her fingers, making her feel almost small.

Tiffany was tall for a woman, so it was definitely not the norm.

She wondered what it'd be like to have his broad shoulders under her fingers, his lean yet muscled body on top of hers.

What would it be like to have his dragon come out to play, to take her a little roughly?

Heat shot through her body, and wetness rushed between her thighs.

Apparently she liked the idea.

Not that she could do anything about it.

Although, if she won, she could claim a prize. Would one kiss hurt? He would've told her about being his true mate—and hadn't said a word—and it could tell her if she was merely horny from being around so many sexy dragonmen or if it were this one man in particular.

True, it could make the remaining days of the orphan event awkward. However, she'd go back to PineRock at the end of it and wouldn't have to see David again.

So would it really be that bad? From everything she knew, David was honorable and wouldn't send her away just because he felt like it. He'd allow her to help until the end.

Of course, to try any of that, she had to win.

Pushing thoughts of a naked David out of her mind, she focused on the dragonwoman at the rock wall and listened to her explanations about the gear.

After all, Tiffany had to win first, and only then could she ask for her boon.

And if she did succeed, then maybe she'd take a chance for once with a man and see if her bad luck with guys had changed.

Chapter Six

As David watched Maya do her final check of Tiffany's safety harness, he warred with what to do. He wanted to win, and yet he also wanted to see what Tiffany claimed as her prize.

They hadn't had a chance to discuss the bet, but for some reason, that only excited him. Not much surprised him these days. And if he were honest with himself, he'd love one.

His dragon spoke up. *But if we win, we could claim a prize. Maybe we could take her to one of the hidden clearings and drive her crazy without so much as touching her, to the point she begs for a kiss and maybe our cock.*

No matter how much you pressure me, I won't kiss her without telling her the truth.

So tell her.

He watched as Tiffany got into position on the other side of the wall. What would her reaction be?

She'd never answered his question about wanting a dragon mate, and it hadn't felt right to bring it up again.

Then she grinned at him and said, "Ready to lose?"

Her mood was infectious, and he smiled back at her. "Does that mean you don't need a head start?"

She snorted. "Hell yes, I'll take it. I'm out to win and need every advantage I can get. I'm competitive but not stupid. A dragon-shifter could beat me at just about everything."

Tiffany's cheeks were already flushed from excitement—would she flush everywhere, if given the reason?—and it took him a second to focus his mind enough to reply, "Okay, then you get ten seconds before I come up after you. I'll pass you soon after and maybe have enough time to take a nap on the ledge up there while I wait for you to catch up."

She rubbed her hands together. "Bring it on, dragonman."

He could feel Maya studying them, but David didn't care. The dragonwoman was a trusted Protector and would never spread rumors or share gossip about how David acted with this human.

Although he had a feeling if he kept acting this way around the female, the entire clan would guess she was his true mate.

Good, his dragon stated.

Not wanting to get distracted, he shushed his

inner beast and nodded at Maya. "I'm ready if Tiffany is."

The human placed her hands on starting grips. "Oh, I'm more than ready."

Maya adjusted her hold on the ropes attached to Tiffany's harness. "Then on my mark. Three, two, one, GO!"

Tiffany scaled up the wall quickly. And if it weren't for the way her ass moved and jiggled as she went, he might've noticed her skill.

But all he could do was imagine stripping her tight shorts off, ripping her panties, and then putting her on her hands and knees on the ledge above, lightly smacking her fine ass as he claimed her hot, wet pussy over and over again, until she screamed his name.

"David! David? Did you hear me? Go!"

He took a second to realize Maya had said anything and cursed. His sex fantasy was going to cost him.

Up the wall he went, instinctively moving his hands and feet in a rhythm that propelled him up the wall without losing his grip or balance.

Tiffany was farther ahead than he'd thought, but he was gaining on her. He pushed his muscles harder, increasing his speed a little, closing the gap between them.

He'd nearly caught up to her when fabric tore, and all of a sudden, black lace peeked through her shorts, showing a bit of skin, and he missed the next grip.

It took him a second to regain his hold and not fall down.

However, by the time he'd done so, Tiffany had climbed up to the ledge and let out a whoop.

He'd...lost.

Although not completely. The glimpse of her lacy panties had been worth it.

He slowly scaled the last bit and pulled himself up on the ledge.

The triumph in her eyes did something to his insides, warming him all over. He liked her being happy.

Even if it meant he'd lost.

She did a little dance. "I won!"

He couldn't help but smile. "You did, Tiffany. So what's your prize?"

"This."

Before he could say anything, she stood on her tiptoes and pressed her lips to his.

For a split second, he groaned at the taste of female and something sweet—cookies, maybe?— before desire surged through him, the need to fuck her flooding his body.

His dragon hummed. *Yes, she's ours. I told you. Rip off those shorts and fuck her here, over and over again. Then we'll take her home and do it some more, until she carries our child.*

Tiffany leaned against him, opening her lips to deepen the kiss, but somehow David found the strength to push her away as he created a temporary mental prison for his dragon. One that would give him a precious few minutes—five at most—before his beast burst free and did everything he could to claim their true mate.

He hated the confusion in her eyes, but he didn't have time to soothe her. He warned, "Run, Tiffany. Gather your stuff, go back to PineRock and stay far away from me."

She searched his gaze. "What are you talking about?"

His dragon beat against the prison, but it still held. "You're my true mate and you kissed me. So unless you want my dragon to claim you and give you a baby, run. And quickly. I can't hold him off much longer."

His dragon thrashed harder, not wanting to let their female go.

Only because David was strong could he keep his beast in check this long after Tiffany's kiss.

She stood there, and he growled. "I mean it, run."

"What if I don't want to?"

Her words floored him, but he recovered quickly. "You may think you don't, but you should. Being with me will put you in danger. Go home and talk with Wes. He'll help you."

The damn female stood there and then placed a hand on his chest. His beast roared even louder.

David gritted his teeth as she said, "No. Tell me what to do." He was about to warn her again when she stood taller. "Don't tell me what I want. Just tell me what I need to do."

As his dragon rammed against the mental prison, David knew he had maybe a minute, two at the most.

So he gave the last type of warning he could. "Go with Maya, and the Protectors will keep you safe."

"Do you want me?"

Despite every reason that he should lie, he said, "Yes."

"Good. Then I'll go with Maya, but I'll be waiting at your house for when you're ready."

As she signaled she was going to descend via the ropes, David watched Tiffany sail down and then talk with Maya. The dragonwoman had probably heard every word already but looked to him and nodded.

If Tiffany was indeed going to his house, he wouldn't be able to fight his dragon.

Fuck. He was both happy and scared shitless about what could happen.

With what precious minutes of control he had left, he took out his cell phone, dialed Wes Dalton, and asked for the biggest damn favor of his life.

TIFFANY PACED THE BEDROOM, the long bathrobe wrapped around her, and wondered where the hell David was.

While she'd been shocked at finding out she was his true mate at first, the offer to go with the frenzy had just spilled from her lips.

And even now, however minutes later, she didn't regret it.

There was something about David that drew her to him. And yes, it would've been nice if he'd told her about the true mate business earlier. However, the truth had put many of his actions into focus—the cautiousness, trying to put distance between them, and the way he hid any flashes of heat from her.

Megan had been the one to give her a quick lesson in what the frenzy would entail. And while the dragonwoman said David had his reasons for not telling her the full truth, it wasn't her story to tell. David would have to share the tale when he was ready.

But regardless, the way he cared for his clan, the way he treated her as an equal, and most definitely how her body had set fire at his kiss…well, all of that made her want a chance with him. Her brother had taken a chance with Gabby without knowing her barely at all in the beginning. Tiffany had decided to do the same.

She glanced at the time again. It'd been nearly an

hour since she'd kissed David. Where was he? From all accounts, he should've found her by now.

Then she heard the front door open and shut. Heavy steps came up the stairs, and her heart rate kicked up.

A few seconds later, David stood in the doorway.

His hair was tousled, his pupils kept flashing, and he stared at her with such longing that she couldn't help but shiver.

Tonight she'd discover the man beneath the usually collected dragon leader.

And she couldn't wait.

His voice was strained as he asked, "Are you sure about this, Tiffany? Once I cross this room, you're mine."

At his possessive tone, her nipples hardened, and wetness rushed between her thighs. His nostrils flared, and she tried not to be embarrassed.

Even without a word, he knew she was aroused.

"Yes, but on one condition."

He clenched his jaw and somehow bit out, "What?"

"That you don't close off from me again. From here on out, you tell me the truth and let me in. I know it'll take time to trust me, but I want you, David. Not the clan leader, not the dragonman trying to uphold some kind of honor. Just you, the man."

With a growl, he stalked across the room and hauled her up against his chest. She sucked in a breath at the heat of his body, his hard muscles, and his even harder cock pressed against her. "You're my true mate, Tiffany. I don't want to hide from you any longer."

Pressing her hands on his chest, she tilted her chin up. "Then kiss me, David. And claim me in the way you need to."

With a groan, his lips crushed against hers, and she instantly parted her lips, his tongue slipping inside.

She moaned as his hot tongue stroked against hers, his taste even better than the quick kiss back at the rock wall.

Moving her hands to his neck, she pressed her breasts against him, needing to feel more of his heat around her.

David gripped her ass and rocked her against him, the friction against her clit making her pussy even wetter.

With a growl, he broke the kiss, ripped off her robe, and pressed her back against his bed.

He shucked his own clothes before crawling over her, kissing his way up her belly, her breasts, suckling one nipple and then the other, before taking her lips again.

Tiffany threaded her fingers through his hair, arching her back, wanting more than kisses from the dragonman above her.

His hand found her pussy, and she hissed as he

lightly stroked her, sending more heat throughout her body.

David whispered, "You're so fucking wet for me already, Tiff." He gently pushed his finger inside, and she arched against him, trying to take him deeper. "I don't have time to lick this sweet cunt right now, but as soon as the frenzy is over, I'll worship you as you deserve, my queen."

She smiled a moment at his reference to their earlier conversation.

But then his thumb found her clit, and any sort of witty remark died on her tongue.

He watched her face as he teased, stroked, and rubbed her most sensitive place. She tried to bring his head down for a kiss, but he shook his head. "Let me watch the first time. I want to see you break apart as you come."

Biting her bottom lip, she nodded and did her best to keep her eyes open. Although as he started to rub harder, with just the amount of pressure she liked, it took everything she had not to close her eyes.

"Are you close, Tiff?"

"Yes."

"Then come for me before I take you with my cock."

She thought it ridiculous he would command such a thing, but as he pressed against her clit, hard, she cried out, and pleasure rushed through her body at the same time her pussy clenched and released his finger inside her.

When she finally relaxed on the bed, he kissed her gently before pulling back and removing his finger. Watching her, he slowly licked her essence off his digit with relish, his pupils flashing rapidly.

Despite her recent orgasm, she grew even wetter.

His husky voice rolled over her as he said, "I can't wait to eat more of that fine honey. But for now, it's time to claim you with my dick and start the frenzy before my dragon tries to take control."

He positioned himself at her entrance, and she instinctively widened her legs, welcoming him.

As he hesitated a second, she blurted, "I'm not a virgin, so just do it."

He smiled, making his eyes so damn sexy, and he said, "When this is all over, I think I'll teach you some patience, my queen. I know how you like games."

The thought of David teasing her, bringing her to the edge only to pull back and start again, made her squirm. "Only if I can do games of my own."

He lowered his face closer to hers. "Anything you want, Tiff. You're mine as much as I'll be yours. That's how true mates work."

With that, he thrust into her to the hilt, and she groaned at how full she was, him stretching her in a good way.

As he started to move, she found her own rhythm

to meet him thrust for thrust, holding onto his shoulders with her hands.

His pupils began to flash quicker, meaning his dragon was closer to gaining control.

But she didn't care. And as he moved his hips faster, she forgot about everything but David's cock reaching inside her, hitting just the right spot, making her want him to claim her in every way possible, not stopping until they both collapsed.

He took her lips in a bruising kiss, his tongue claiming her mouth as his cock claimed her pussy. When his fingers found her clit again, she cried out, pleasure exploding, David never stopping his hips, the movement spiraling her into pure bliss.

With a growl, he finally stilled, and as he orgasmed, it sent her into another of her own, the pleasure almost too much, making her back arch.

When she finally came down from her high, David stared at her with slitted pupils, desire flaming in his gaze.

His dragon was in control.

And despite the fact he'd already given her two orgasms, her cunt throbbed, wanting more.

David's voice was a little deeper as he said, "Now it's my turn to claim you." He pulled out, flipped her over on her stomach, and lifted her hips. In the next second, his cock thrust into her, and she moaned.

She knew the dragon only half cared about her

orgasm at this point, needing to brand her with his seed.

So she merely met his frantic thrusts, loving how his balls hit against her pussy, the sound of sex and flesh filling the room.

When he thrust harder, he bit out, "You're mine, Tiffany Ford. All mine. Take my cock and come for me."

Then his finger found her clit, and he flicked his nail against her sensitive bud. Tiffany screamed as she orgasmed again, David stilling at the same time, his release pushing her ever closer to where the pleasure was too much.

Like she might die from it.

A few beats later, her hair was brushed off her neck, and David kissed her nape. He said, "Are you okay, Tiff?"

He pulled out before slowly turning her around and caressing her jaw. His pupils were round, with no sign of flashing. She blurted, "What about your dragon?"

He smiled, the sight making her heart skip a beat. Again. Damn the man, he affected her like no other guy before. He replied, "Even he knows you need rest sometimes, especially since you're human." He lay next to her and pulled her half on his chest. "And he's going to allow me to explain a few things to you, to hopefully make this easier."

She propped her chin on his chest and met his

gaze. "If the two times so far are any indication, I think we're doing just fine."

He chuckled, and the sound made her heart warm. David looked more relaxed, more like just a man, unburdened with so many responsibilities.

Which made her want to know him all the more.

He brushed hair off her forehead before saying, "Sex most definitely won't be a problem." His voice turned husky. "In fact, I can't wait to be inside you again."

She smiled at his tone and lightly rubbed her hand against his smooth chest. "Just as soon as you explain why you didn't tell me I was your true mate."

He let out a sigh. "That didn't take long for you to ask, huh?"

She raised an eyebrow. "That's not an answer."

He smiled again. "No, it's not. And never stop trying to get the truth from me because I'll admit, it's not always easy for me to give."

"Because you're clan leader?"

He nodded. "Mostly, yes." As he lightly caressed her cheek, Tiffany leaned into his touch. It would be so easy to kiss him again and focus on the frenzy.

But she wanted this answer first. So she pushed on. "Then tell me."

David continued to play with a few strands of her hair as he answered, "Because I was trying to protect you."

She frowned. "From what? As we've established

earlier, I'm not exactly the wilting violet type. And you know from my volunteer application that I've taken all kinds of self-defense training back on PineRock."

He shook his head. "It's not that." He paused a beat before continuing, "The last five mates of StoneRiver's clan leaders all died within a few years of being mated. My uncle was the former clan leader and was one of those five. So he warned me and Justin from a young age to watch out and to learn from his pain."

Well, then. She definitely needed more information. "How did they die?"

"A combination of accidents and murder."

Her first instinct was to brush it aside as coincidences he'd tried to make sense of. However, she sensed this was a huge deal to David. Otherwise he would've told her that he was her true mate.

So Tiffany decided to approach it from a more rational standpoint. "Accidents are out of our control, though, right? So if you take those out, how many were murdered?"

"Two."

"Well, that's better odds. Not that I'm dismissing their deaths or the pain it caused. But just that until recent years, dragon-shifters had a tough time with poachers and those out to destroy you. I'm sure other clans in the Tahoe area had some misfortune as a result, too. Right?"

He frowned. "Well, someone from SkyTree was murdered about twenty years ago. Those poaching dragon's blood captured the clan leader's mate."

"Was that around the same time as when one of the StoneRiver clan leader mates were murdered?"

He answered slowly, "Yes."

"So it wasn't just StoneRiver's bad luck, or what have you."

His brows drew together, as if trying to convince himself it was true.

Scooting up until her face was even with his, she cupped his cheek and said, "While I can never rule out accidents, I think we can try our best to prevent murder. Between your protection and any and all training I can take to defend myself, we can ensure this clan leader's mate doesn't end up the same way."

Oh, crap. He hadn't actually asked her to mate him yet. But the words were out, and she wasn't going to take them back.

As she stared into his dark brown eyes, Tiffany waited. If he didn't believe her now, about how they could stop the chain of bad luck, she'd keep working on it. Because as long as he feared for her constantly, it would forever keep a part of him from her.

And from what she'd already learned of the dragonman, about his kindness, loyalty, and even a small hint of humor, she wanted to know more. Much more.

That wasn't the only reason, though. If David

continuously believed she was a step away from dying, he might try to keep her contained on StoneRiver and make her miserable in the long run. She didn't need complete freedom, but nor did she want to be a prisoner for the rest of her life.

However, she couldn't think of any next steps until David said something. So she waited for his reply, to see what came next.

DAVID'S DRAGON paced inside his mind, making it hard to focus solely on Tiffany and their conversation.

And yet he knew his dragon was showing extreme restraint, letting him have this break with their female so soon.

But it'd been the bargain he'd made with his beast, to go through with the frenzy at all. That after they'd both had her once, he'd get some time to explain things to her.

Although David would be lying if he didn't want to spread Tiffany below him right then and there and take her again. Because damn, she'd been better than he ever could've imagined. Even now, when he knew he needed to tell her the truth behind keeping the secret, all he could think about was kissing her as he fucked her again.

However, once she laid out a rational explanation

for the murders and accidents, he could do nothing but focus on her face and words.

And when she put together a plan of how to keep her safe, she wormed her way a little into his heart.

His female wasn't one to merely let things happen to her. No, she would help craft a future she wanted and fight for it.

So far, it seemed as if fate had been right in making her his true mate.

He finally replied, "With barely any time to come up with a solution, you've already got an ad hoc plan in place." He caressed her jaw. "You're so damn amazing and make me think we have a chance." David threaded his fingers through her hair as she blushed. He added, "And while we can't iron it all out right now—my dragon and I are anxious to keep going with the frenzy—it's a good start." He brought her face closer to his. "Once the frenzy is over, we'll work on this. Together. And find a solution so that you're around for many, many years to come."

She relaxed a fraction and nodded. "Okay, sounds like a plan. As long as you don't try to make me into one of those princesses hidden away from the world, unable to help with her own destiny, I think we'll make it work."

The idea of Tiffany being locked up, unable to see her brother or even the friends she'd made, made him frown. "I wouldn't do that. As long as we're both honest and have common sense, we can make a go at this and find something that works to please both you and my inner dragon."

"And what about the man part of you?"

He nuzzled her cheek. "He's going to need a little more time with you naked and in his bed before he can think of anything else."

She laughed and leaned until her breast brushed his shoulder. David sucked in a breath as his dragon growled, *She's had a rest. I want her again. Hurry up, or I won't take turns and will just fuck her until I get tired.*

No, you wouldn't hurt her like that.

Maybe not. But I wouldn't waste so much damn time talking.

At his dragon's petulant tone, he snorted. Tiffany raised her brows in question, and he said, "You may not realize how much restraint my dragon has right now, letting me talk to you so soon, but it's a lot. I hope it's enough for a while, as the frenzy is going to start up again soon."

Leaning her nipple and breast even more against him, she murmured, "I'm anxious to get to it again myself."

With a growl, he rolled her over and pinned her hands above her head. His lips stopped an inch from hers as he said, "Good. Because it's time to claim you as mine again."

She brushed her foot against the back of his calf. "Then take me, dragonman. I'm waiting."

With a growl, he took her lips in a fierce kiss as he

released her hands. As he tweaked one nipple, he used his other arm to position his cock and slide home.

And so David went about claiming his true mate over and over again, taking turns with his beast, enjoying his beautiful, playful, and smart female, never quite sure how he deserved her. And yet, he refused to give her up. Ever.

Chapter Seven

Tiffany lost track of the days as they had sex, rested, ate, and talked. David had turned out to have more humor than she'd first realized, but her greatest discovery had been in finding out he was ticklish. And she'd relished in making him laugh uncontrollably.

Sure, it was a little childish. But she rather thought that was exactly what David needed in his life—the chance to relax and let go with someone.

With her.

It was too much to ask for him to trust her completely this soon. But whenever they rested to eat or shower, he'd regularly brought up her idea about preventing a repeat of what had happened to the other StoneRiver leader mates.

Well, they'd managed to talk some, at any rate.

Truth be told, not much talking had gotten done in the shower either.

Sleep, however, had been necessary. And as she awoke to sunshine streaming in from the window, she noticed David facing her on the bed, staring at her. She yawned and asked, "Were you watching me sleep again?"

He traced her cheek and wiped away the drop of drool from the corner of her mouth, and smiled. "I was waiting to see how long it would take for the spit to reach the pillow."

She pushed playfully against his chest. "That's not very flattering."

He raised his brows. "Why? It sat there for a really long time. It must be because it's as attached to your lips as I am."

Before she could reply, he leaned over and kissed her lips gently. He took his time nibbling her bottom lip before slowly exploring her mouth. As if he were a magnet and her a piece of metal, she moved until her body was pressed to his and kissed him back.

She had fully expected for him to reach between her legs and make sure she was nice and wet for their next round. However, he merely pulled away and touched his nose to hers. His pupils flashed a few times, and she asked, "Are you having some sort of test with your dragon, to see how long you can keep him restrained before he takes over?"

Not that Tiffany minded. It was a game David

had played with his beast. And, well, when the dragon broke free, it showed a rather animalistic side to sex she admitted liking.

He traced her cheek. "As much as your blush tells me you'd like that, no. It's something else." Cupping her jaw, he added, "The frenzy is over, Tiffany. You carry my babe."

For a second, she tried to process the information. Of course she knew it was the aim of the whole mate-claim frenzy.

And yet, it had been in the abstract. Now, there was a life taking root inside her.

Something that was a part of her and a part of David.

A little boy or girl that would bind them together forever.

As his thumb caressed her cheek, he asked, "Are you okay?"

She met his eyes again and smiled. "Of course. It's just…weird. Like, I knew it would happen. And yet, it's still strange to think I'm going to be a mom in the not-too-distant future."

He took her hand, threaded his fingers through hers, and murmured, "I'll be there, too, love. We'll do this together."

At the surety in his voice, the edge of nervousness faded. Even if they hadn't known each other long, there was something about David that made her want to trust him. Implicitly.

Hitching a leg over his hip, she leaned into him and took his lips for a quick kiss. "I know you will be. If anything, I suspect you'll be the overprotective one."

He put his arm over her waist until his fingers splayed her back. "Dragon-shifters, in general, are like that. I'm sure your sister-in-law is the same way?"

She raised an eyebrow. "You clearly don't know my brother Ryan very well. He puts most dragons to shame when it comes to protecting his son."

He smiled. "Well, then that just means he and I can team up and protect both our children, across the clans then."

Tiffany hesitated a second, wanting to ask him about clan matters but unsure if she should.

Yes, she and David had just finished a sex marathon and would have a baby. But she didn't know if he'd share more delicate clan matters with her yet.

As if reading her mind, he gently forced her to meet his gaze again. "Tell me whatever's on your mind, Tiff. I may have fucked up by keeping the truth about being true mates from you, but it's only honesty going forward."

She bit the bullet and blurted, "You're going to have to form a closer alliance with PineRock because of me, aren't you?"

He smiled and stroked her back in slow circles. "It

was in the works beforehand, love. Being with you will just hurry it along a little."

She searched his gaze. "Are you okay with that? I don't like to think I'm forcing you to lead the clan in a way you don't want to."

He took her face between his hands. "It's true. It probably would've taken another year or two to ask for a close alliance with PineRock. But Wes has proven a useful ally already. When I asked him to take over the orphan event so I could go through with the frenzy, he didn't hesitate to jump in. He even kept me updated, for when I could check emails the few times you were sleeping." He strummed his thumbs against her skin, and she relaxed a fraction. "If anything, you've made this all smoother, and I should be thanking you for kissing me at the rock wall."

His words eased the worry she'd had about interfering and causing trouble. "If however many days of sex was the reward for that win, it makes me wonder what the boon will be for the next wager. Because it has to top it, of course."

He chuckled, the sound making her grin. She'd never tire of his laugh. He replied, "Well, you can ask me to take you up into the air in my dragon form. That might come close."

Her eyes widened. "Really? I didn't know you could do that. I'm sure my brother has had Gabby take him into the air before, although he'd never own up to it. Especially since I think it's illegal, right?"

David nodded. "Technically, yes, it is. We're not supposed to carry humans into the air. But you'll be my mate soon, Tiffany. So things are different. Well, provided you agree to be my mate." His pupils flickered. "Will you?"

She stared into his dark brown eyes and saw the brief vulnerability there. The strong clan leader wasn't as confident about all things, it seemed.

Best to squash any doubts. It may not have been long, but being with David was just…right.

She answered, "Wild horses couldn't stop me."

He took her lips in a slow kiss, devouring her mouth as if it were the first time. Licking, tasting, making her groan at how one man could make her so hot and wet, and a million other things at the same time.

His hand found her pussy and lightly stroked. Not caring if she was a little sore, she moved toward his fingers, loving how he teased and traced and lightly thrust into her.

He broke the kiss and growled, "I love how wet you get for me."

"Only for you, David. Only for you."

With a groan, he slid his cock into her and placed her leg higher over his hip, giving him more access to her as they lay facing each other on their sides.

They stared into one another's eyes as he moved

slowly this time. She met his thrusts, both of them taking their time to enjoy each other and—at least in Tiffany's case—wishing they could stay like this for a little while longer.

But she pushed aside the thought about how their little bubble of two would break soon enough and instead gripped David's shoulder. When she dug in her nails, he moaned and increased his pace.

The leisurely movements turned frantic, and he finally kissed her again, taking her mouth with the same need as her pussy, almost as if he were trying to tell her how much she meant to him already.

Then he brushed her clit, and her orgasm crashed over her, sending pleasure through her body just as David stilled and found his own.

With each jet of release, she went over the edge again, until she finally lay there, spent and breathing hard.

David took her lips in a slow, possessive kiss before breaking it and saying, "You're mine, Tiffany Ford. And we'll make it official as soon as possible."

She ran her fingers against his jaw. "I think Tiffany Lee might be better, don't you think?"

His pupils flashed before he kissed her again.

And he claimed her one more time before they both showered and readied themselves to face the world once more.

Chapter Eight

After finally emerging from his home for the first time in nearly two weeks, David spent the rest of the day dealing with clan disputes, leftover paperwork, and reading the reports Wes had left for the dragon orphan event.

And while that kept him busy, the biggest surprise of all had come from Justin and Megan—they'd put in an application to adopt Madison.

While he knew they'd always longed for a daughter and had given up after three tries, he hadn't thought they would add a fourth child to their family. But he was happy to be wrong for once, as the little girl would be loved and spoiled, as she should be. Not to mention his nephew Andy already seemed attached to her as well.

By that evening, he and Tiffany had merely

crashed into bed and conked out, too tired to do much else.

As David watched his female make breakfast in the morning, there was a knock on the front door.

His dragon yawned. *It's too early for visitors.*

It may not be a visitor. Something could've happened.

His beast grumbled. *I was happy to watch Tiffany's ass as she moved about the kitchen.*

Me too, dragon. But in a few days she'll officially be our mate, and we'll have decades to do so.

Ignoring his inner beast's pouts, he checked the peephole on the front door and resisted a groan. He'd expected Tiffany's brother to show up, but not quite so soon.

Standing a little straighter, he opened the door to a tall, frowning male with the same dark hair and hazel eyes as Tiffany, a slightly shorter dragonwoman standing at his side. The human growled, "Where's my sister?"

The dragonwoman with brown eyes and light brown skin at his side rolled her eyes. "Hello, David. I don't know if you remember me, but I'm Gabby Santos-Ford. This is my mate, Ryan. I tried to get him to wait for a decent hour, but he wouldn't listen."

He nodded at Gabby—he'd met her once before but didn't remember where—and then focused on Ryan. "Won't you come in?"

The human narrowed his eyes. "It's the least you could do, given what you did to my sister."

His dragon growled, but Tiffany appeared at his side before David could say a word. She poked Ryan in the chest. "Be nice to David. He didn't do anything to me that I didn't want done. Do you really want me to go into detail about all I instigated? Hell, what I asked for him to do to me?"

Ryan frowned as his mate, Gabby, bit her lip to keep from laughing. The human male muttered, "I don't need the details."

David merely stood there with a smug smile, loving how Tiffany didn't shy from her attraction to him.

Or, maybe more. But he wasn't going to think of that right now.

Tiffany nodded. "Good. I just finished making some bacon and eggs. If you can be civil to my future mate, then you can come in. Otherwise, Gabby can join us, and you can wait out there until you calm down."

Ryan replied, "I'm your older brother, Tiffany. You're supposed to listen to me."

Tiffany raised her brows. "Oh, really? Considering you wouldn't be here right now at all if I hadn't nudged you to enter the dragon lottery, I rather think I've earned the right to make my own decisions."

Gabby murmured something into Ryan's ear that David couldn't hear, and the human finally sighed. "I'll be nice. Let's just say it's been a shock, is all."

Tiffany leaned against David's side, and he put an arm around her as he said, "So how about we start over?" He put his hand out to shake. "Call me David. It's nice to meet you."

Ryan shook his hand, gave him one last older brother glare that didn't faze David one bit, and the human released his hand.

His dragon said, *Challenge him to something later. Maybe if there's a competition that won't end in fists flying, it might help ease his protectiveness and see us as something other than the male who fucked his sister.*

Maybe. Let's get through this morning first.

Tiffany motioned inside, and they all followed her to the kitchen.

As soon as they sat at the counter, Gabby asked, "So when's the mating ceremony?"

Ryan grunted. "You don't know that they'll have one."

Gabby met David's gaze, smiled at what she saw, and tilted her head a fraction to the side. "Somehow, I think there will be. And sooner rather than later too."

He nodded. "Tiffany agreed to be my mate. We're just waiting for ADDA to make the final approval."

Gabby swiped a strawberry from a bowl on the counter and said, "I'm sure Ashley's helping with that."

Ryan sighed. "Considering how she took the

ADDA employees to task about letting that couple slip through the application process—and yes, word of that has spread through PineRock as well—I don't know if her help will matter."

David said, "I would've done the same thing if I had the connection to ADDA that Ashley does. If not for Tiff noticing, who knows what could've happened."

Tiffany placed the plate and bowl with the bacon and eggs on the counter. "You would've noticed as well, David." She hesitated a beat, and he didn't like it. Finally she said, "But you'll have an extra set of eyes to help you now, when you need it."

He understood the cause of her hesitation and decided to put an end to it.

Not caring if her brother was sitting in the same room, he went over to her and cupped her cheek. "I'll always want your help, Tiffany. I may be clan leader, but I'm not invincible. And heaven knows I need more eyes and ears, especially if we keep trying to do these types of events with the orphans."

She smiled up at him. "I'll give you a report each time." She stood on her tiptoes to whisper into his ear, "To help make up for the one I never did for you."

He murmured back, "I'm sure it'd be a hell of a lot more thorough now than before."

She laughed, and he couldn't help but kiss her. Not as long as he liked, given how her brother sighed loudly, but at least enough to promise he'd do much more later.

He pulled back, and Gabby grinned at them before nudging her mate. "I told you there was a softie inside the clan leader."

David frowned. "I'm not soft."

Gabby replied, "I mean no offense. But with your female, you most definitely are."

He grunted, but Tiffany replied before he could, "Most dragon-shifters are with their mates." She took a plate and dished out some food before handing it to him. She added, "So how long are you two staying on StoneRiver?"

As they all ate breakfast and Ryan and Gabby shared they'd only be there for part of the day and then went on to give advice about Tiffany and David's forthcoming child, David was content to sit next to his mate and keep his thigh pressed against hers.

He had a number of clan leader duties to do later. But for now, he enjoyed the glimpse of what his life would be like in the future, a mate by his side and never facing the day alone again.

She laughed at something Gabby said, and a sense of rightness settled over him. David wondered how the hell he ever thought it'd be best to push Tiffany away. She made everything brighter, lighter, and fun.

Still, he needed to ensure she kept up her training

and could protect herself. Because he wasn't going to chance anything happening to her. His fears about her being stolen from him had lessened but weren't completely gone.

And he wasn't going to lose her if he could help it.

Chapter Nine

After her brother and his mate left and returned to PineRock, David headed to the Protectors' building, and Tiffany was left alone.

Not that she usually minded her own company. But it only reinforced what she'd been trying to avoid thinking about—she didn't have a place within the clan. At least, not yet.

Helping her brother after his ex-wife left him had taken up a lot of her energy for years. Then he'd found Gabby, and she'd worked hard to find a way to live near her brother on PineRock.

Then she'd found a job helping at the bar and restaurant that catered to both humans and dragon-shifters.

And while she wanted to go back to work there, David said not yet. Until she was officially his mate and he could ensure she was ready to defend herself against enemies—especially if the League got word of their mating and she became a target— she had to stay within the boundaries of StoneRiver.

But sitting around wasn't really her style. So she decided to head out for a run instead.

Exploring StoneRiver on her own did wonders to ease her restlessness. She didn't know many people inside the clan yet, but word had spread of her and David. So everyone waved at her, and a few kids had even stopped her a couple of times to ask some questions.

For the most part, StoneRiver seemed like its clan members were content. Oh, a few people—especially older dragon-shifters—ignored her. But she could handle that. After all, it wasn't as if humans had been overly welcome to dragons over the centuries. Much like she and her brother had come to know and accept dragon-shifters, in time, she hoped they would reciprocate the feeling and at least give Tiffany a chance.

She'd just made the turn toward Megan and Justin's house when she spotted Maya, the Protector she'd first met at the rock wall before the frenzy.

Just as Tiffany dropped to a walk, the dragonwoman reached her, and they both stopped in place. "Good, I found you."

She frowned. "Is something wrong?"

"Oh, no. It's just that ADDA and some human

police never got the chance to talk to you about the Utah dragon couple and are here now."

She glanced down at her shorts and tank. "I'm not exactly fit for a formal interview."

Maya bit her lip and then said, "You should just come straight away. They're already irritated about having to wait until the frenzy is over. And until your mating is official, you probably shouldn't do anything to upset ADDA."

She knew from living with PineRock that it greatly depended on who you met from ADDA as to how your experience went.

And in case she ended up with one of the grumpy ones, it was best to not keep them waiting. "All right then, let's go."

She was able to grab a quick drink of water inside the Protector building and freshen up in the restroom before being guided into the visitor's room.

Inside sat three men, one in a suit and tie and the other two in police uniforms. The two police officers stood as soon as she entered, but the man in the suit merely gestured to the seat across from her. "Thank you for coming. This shouldn't take long."

Even though Tiffany had little reason to interact with ADDA much after she'd been granted permission to live near her brother, it was odd they'd sent a man. Most of the time, they sent a woman to deal with dragon mates. It'd always been the case for her brother.

Of course, she wasn't a dragon mate yet, she told herself.

Sitting down, she asked, "What can I do for you guys?"

The man in a suit replied, "We merely need your statement concerning Mr. and Mrs. Dunn to add to the report." He adjusted a notepad in front of him and said, "Tell me what happened."

As she recounted the events, she kept looking over at the police. They both studied her with an intensity that didn't make sense considering she wasn't the child predator but merely the witness to a pair of them.

When she finished, the ADDA man said, "That's a good start. We'll need you to come to the Reno office to identify the couple and sign some paperwork."

She frowned. "Is that really necessary? I could easily pick them out from a bunch of photos, if you bring them here."

The man shook his head. "That won't be quite enough. Having a human confirm the identities in person will strengthen the case."

Tiffany wasn't stupid, and it all seemed like a lot of unnecessary footwork. "I'm not sure how me picking them out from a book of pictures versus a lineup will make that much difference."

The man across from her shifted a little in his seat. And she swore his brow was a little sweaty.

Why would he be nervous? ADDA employees conducted interviews all the time.

A quick glance at the two cops revealed nothing about them, though. They merely had blank expressions trained on her.

Before she could think much more on it, he said, "Handling dragon-shifters across state lines can be tricky. I want to make it as much an open and shut case as possible. Having video of you confirming their identities in person will leave no doubt as to who you saw interacting with the little dragon girl." As she thought about protesting some more, the man added, "Doing this means ADDA would approve your mating request. If you don't cooperate, then it may be denied."

She barely resisted a frown. As far as she knew, it was basically a foregone conclusion that her and David's request would be granted. After all, she was pregnant with a dragon-shifter's child, and all half-dragon children had to live with a dragon clan.

"So let's be off." The man stood. "Leaving now means you should be back before dinner time."

She stood as well. "I need to talk to David and change clothes first."

He shook his head. "David isn't here right now. I know because I tried to get an interview with him before you."

The warning bells inside her head only grew louder. David had said nothing about leaving the clan's land. Granted, they were newly together, but she sensed he would've mentioned leaving StoneRiver to her.

Unless it was some sort of emergency. Of course there was an easy way to verify that.

Not wanting to let the men know she suspected anything, she shrugged. "I'll just tell the head Protector. As long as he clears it, I'll go with you."

The man in the suit looked to say something, but one of the cops spoke up. "You have five minutes. Otherwise, if we wait much longer, our superior won't be there when we get to Reno. And he wants this information by four o'clock today."

With a nod, she exited the room to find Maya still waiting. Keeping her voice low, Tiffany asked, "Did David leave StoneRiver today?"

She nodded. "He had to go check something in the nearby woods. A group of humans was spotted who shouldn't have been there."

At Maya's words, her tension eased a little. In an emergency, she'd want David to check it out instead of merely taking time to tell her.

So she said, "They want me to go to Reno to ID the couple. I need to talk with Jon."

Maya shook her head. "He's with David. Zed's in charge."

Tiffany resisted a groan. Zed was the oldest Protector on StoneRiver and the only one who didn't seem to like her.

Still, she stood tall and stated, "Then let me talk to him and check it's okay to go."

"He already told me that it's fine if they need to take you to Reno."

She muttered, "Probably so he wouldn't have to talk to me."

Maya gently touched her arm. "He's in the minority here, Tiffany. I promise you that."

Smiling at the dragonwoman who was slowly becoming her friend, she nodded. "I know." Taking a deep breath, she added, "Then I'll go with them. Let David and Jon know, as well as Zed. I'll be back by nightfall."

The dragonwoman asked, "Do you have your cell phone with you to call?"

"Damn, I didn't take it on my run today."

Maya put up a finger, dashed to the front reception area, and then came back with a cheap cell phone. "Take this, just in case. The numbers to David, Jon, and the front desk here at the Protector building are all there."

She took the phone and tucked it into her sports bra since she didn't have any pockets. "Thanks. I'll see you tonight."

With a wave, she went back into the room. In the next minute, they were all heading toward a dark SUV and piling inside. Tiffany sat in the back with one of the police officers, while the ADDA employee drove and the other police sat in the front seat.

The man next to her stared at her with an unreadable expression. He couldn't be older than forty, with dark hair streaked with a few strands of silver. She glanced at his badge and saw the name "Jones." Before she could try to memorize his badge number—just in case, she told herself—the ADDA employee spoke up. "Thanks for coming with us, Miss Ford. You made the right choice."

His words were odd-sounding to her. "Of course. I want to keep the Dunns from harming any other children."

A few beats passed, and she noticed they were well down the bumpy road leading to the state road. She thought the conversation was dead when the police officer turned and said, "Not that choice."

Frowning, she struggled to keep her voice civil as she asked, "Then what choice are you talking about?"

The officer replied, "The one where you came with us so we can rid you of your dragon spawn, and the League can help you see the light again."

Her heart skipped a beat and her stomach dropped. "What?"

The man stared down at her breasts a beat before he said, "We have men willing to overlook the fact you've had a dirty dragon dick inside you. Within the week, you'll be free of that demon in your belly and wed to a man who will show you that humans only belong with humans."

Her hand went instinctively to her lower stomach. They wanted to take away her baby and…what? Force her to wed someone to try and brainwash her?

Doing her best to not show her fear—although her heart thumped hard inside her chest—she cleared her throat and focused on the fact she had a phone she could use at the next opportunity. As long as she could contact StoneRiver, David and the others would save her.

It was best to keep them talking and find out what she could. So she asked, "What are you talking about? Who are you?"

The man next to her smiled slowly. "I'm your soon-to-be husband. It was between the pair of us, but as soon as I saw you, I knew you would be mine." He traced her cheek, and bile rose in her throat. "I'll be the one to show you it's best to stick to your own kind."

Focus, Tiff. Don't freak out. You need to stay calm to call David and the others.

And yet, as the man continued touching her face, she struggled to keep her breakfast down. Or to not grab and twist his balls until he cried in pain.

She was in a moving car with three men. It was nearly impossible to escape until they stopped somewhere.

Then she remembered the ADDA employee in the driver's seat, and even though she sensed it would be hopeless, she stated, "If you work for ADDA, then you can't just let them take me."

The man at her side—Jones, if his badge was even real—answered, "Oh, Gerald works for ADDA. But we own him. He'll never talk. He's actually the one who suggested this trip."

She tried to meet Gerald's gaze in the rearview mirror, but the coward kept his eyes on the road.

It seemed even ADDA had League sympathizers within their ranks.

Jones moved his hand to her neck, gripped the back, and as he tightened his fingers, she froze.

If only she wasn't in a car, she'd try to make an escape.

The man raised a cloth she hadn't even noticed he'd been holding and moved it toward her face. "Can't have you running away before we're married."

She finally struggled, doing her best to ignore the pain at his tightened grip, and managed to punch between his thighs.

He hissed, anger flashed in his eyes, and he said, "You'll pay for that later, dragon whore."

In the next second, he put the cloth to her face, and within a few beats, the world went black.

Chapter Ten

After hours of tracking down the college kids who'd thought to camp on StoneRiver's lands as part of a dare, and even more hours dealing with ADDA and the police, all David wanted to do was go home, kiss his female, and fall asleep with her in his arms.

But first, he headed into the Protector building after Jon, needing to check in with Zed, the male they'd left in charge.

He'd barely stepped into the reception area when Maya rushed up to him and Jon. "I need to talk with you two. Come on."

She gestured out the door and then went outside. David looked to Jon, who shrugged. The other male said, "Maya doesn't ask for something without a reason."

Knowing it was true, he nodded and then went

back outside. The dragonwoman stood at the far side of the car park, right before it met the road.

His dragon said, *Something's wrong.*

I agree. But let's find out what it is first.

As soon as he and Jon were standing in front of Maya, she kept her voice low as she said, "It's Tiffany. She left with an ADDA employee and two cops right around noon and hasn't come home. And no, she hasn't called, either."

Since it was close to midnight, Maya's words only made his heart race faster. He wanted to rush out and go look for her. But he couldn't do anything until he knew what had happened. "Tell us everything."

As Maya explained about the visit and Tiffany going to ID the dragon couple, David did his best to focus on the small details. Inside, he was a wreck.

However, his female was smart and a fighter. If something were wrong, he'd have to count on her staying alive long enough for him to find her.

The dragonwoman finally finished with, "And the reason I brought you out here is that, well, I think Zed knew they would take her. And I don't know if any of the others inside helped him."

David narrowed his eyes. "What?"

Maya went on, "Zed told me to let them do whatever they wanted with her. When I asked what it would be, he said he didn't care. And even when I tried to bring up again later how Tiffany should've been back, Zed dismissed it, saying maybe she'd come to her senses and ran away." She bit her lip and added, "I wanted to punch him in the face, but I know there are others who sympathize with him inside the clan and the Protectors. And me going up against him alone would be suicide."

David clenched his fingers into fists, wishing he could punch the male himself. "Did you reach out to Ashley Swift?"

Maya shook her head. "I wanted to but didn't know if I should do it without permission."

Part of him roared at her answer, but the more rational side knew dragon-shifters needed order and hierarchy to survive without killing each other. He quickly blurted, "When it comes to Tiffany, or the safety of any human on StoneRiver, always feel free to reach out to Ashley if needed."

The dragonwoman nodded, and Jon spoke. "We need to talk to Zed and see what he knows about these three males."

He'd known Zed didn't like humans living on StoneRiver but hadn't expected the male to do something so drastic.

However, David wouldn't underestimate the male again. And if Zed had indeed been part of what happened to Tiffany, he'd pummel and banish the male as soon as possible.

His dragon said, *Save the anger for when we find those who took Tiffany. For now, focus.*

Taking a deep breath, David relied on his years

of being in charge and said, "Me and Jon will try to find and talk with Zed. Maya, call Ashley right away. I don't care if it's late. Keep calling until she picks up. Explain the situation and find out what you can about this Gerald White male. Find us as soon as you're done."

Maya put up a hand. "There's one more thing. I gave her one of our Protector phones. If it's still on, we should be able to track it."

The dragonwoman may be young, but David admired her foresight. She'd go far in the clan. He nodded. "Then do that first and then talk to Ashley."

After Maya took out her phone, he met Jon's gaze. The head Protector said, "We'll find her. Don't worry."

With a grunt, David headed back to the building, Jon on his heels.

His dragon paced inside his head, as anxious as he was about Tiffany.

His beast said, *We'll find her. And then we need to rid the clan of any who'd wish her harm.*

He wished he didn't have to think of doing something so drastic. After all, with Tasha mating Brad, the grumbles had barely been anything. But apparently, a human about to mate the clan leader was enough to push the disgruntled over the edge.

David could no longer ignore the problem.

He replied, *Yes, we'll do that. But first, we focus on Tiffany.*

It wasn't long before they reached the office used for the night watch in charge or the Protector left in command anytime Jon had to deal with things away from the clan. David didn't bother to knock but instead turned the knob and entered.

Jeff, the usual lead Protector for the night watch, looked up at them. "Did you finish with those college kids then?"

He didn't bother to answer. "Where's Zed?"

Jeff frowned. "He left two hours ago, when I arrived. Why?"

David knew that Jeff had tried to woo a human server from Tasha's restaurant before. And even though he'd ultimately failed, the male wasn't against humans and dragon-shifters being together.

A quick look at Jon, who nodded in agreement, told him they could trust Jeff.

So he filled the dragonman in, and the three of them came up with a plan on how to look for Zed without raising suspicion.

And as soon as he could, David went looking for Maya, hoping she knew where Tiffany might be.

TIFFANY SLOWLY OPENED her eyes and instantly felt like she needed to throw up.

Even though she rolled to her side to do just that, the feeling eased a bit, and she kept everything down.

It was far too early in her pregnancy to have morning sickness, which meant it was probably a result of whatever they'd dosed her with.

In that second, she realized they could've done anything to her while unconscious.

Like take away her child.

She felt her clothes all in place, even her shoes, and willed herself to believe it was a good sign. While not a guarantee, she didn't think they'd put her back into her running outfit if they'd undressed her and ended her pregnancy.

Taking deep breaths, she tried to calm her heart rate. Despite her pounding head and queasiness, she needed to try and get her wits about her.

Slowly sitting up, she looked around the room. But there was merely a bed, a dresser, and a nightstand with some water bottles on top of it. The walls were some sort of beige color that could be found anywhere. A door was open to the side, showing her a toilet and sink.

In short, it was a bedroom with what looked like a small attached bathroom.

And a glance at the window showed there were outer shutters closed in front of it. With slow steps to keep her stomach settled, Tiffany tried the window, but it wouldn't open.

Not that she'd expected it to. If these men had gone to the trouble of blackmailing an ADDA employee, they weren't going to be that stupid.

Or at least she wouldn't underestimate them.

It was only then that she noticed the small, hard object in her sports bra.

The cell phone.

She quickly took it out, opened the flip phone, and noticed right away there was no service.

Even though it shouldn't surprise her—large swaths of land had patchy service in the forests around Lake Tahoe, if that's indeed where they still were—she sighed and slumped a little.

But in less than a minute, she stood tall and surveyed the room. There was no fucking way she'd give up that easily.

Glancing over the various objects, a plan came together. One that relied on her not being in some sort of unusually tall building.

Rushing to the window, she did her best to look through the small slit in the middle, where the shutters didn't quite meet. By the light of the full moon, she could make out pine trees and mountains in the distance. However, she couldn't see the ground.

So she stood on her tiptoes and tried to see how far up she was.

There. She could see the ground in the distance.

And if she could tie the bedsheets, secure them, break the window, and climb down to a safe enough distance to jump to the ground before they entered the room, she might have a chance.

More so if she could push the dresser in front of the door to stall them.

True, there could be guards around the building, but she had to at least try. David and the others would no doubt be looking for her by now. So if she could make it to the cover of the forest, find a signal, and maybe climb one of the trees to hide, she might, just might be able to escape.

There were a lot of variables to success, but it was her best chance. Her only chance, really, if she wanted to keep her baby. Because the longer she stayed here, the greater chance they'd drug her again and take away her child.

Right, Tiff. You can do this. Now, get to work.

Not wanting to think of how stupid the men had to be to put her in a room with so many objects, Tiffany went to work on the sheets first, knowing she could easily hide them under the comforter if someone came to check on her.

She managed to finish her rope using the thinner under blanket and the sheets from the bed and decided securing it to the bed frame was her best hope.

Just as she was about to crouch down to do that, she heard footsteps outside the door. Quickly, she jumped into the bed, careful to keep the ad hoc rope in her arms, flipped the blanket over her, and feigned sleep.

The door opened, and a male voice muttered, "She's still out. Why don't we just wake her up?"

That had been the man known as Jones.

"Putting more drugs in her system might kill her. I'm fine with that, but you seem to want the bitch."

Jones replied, "I could just rip off her clothes and wake her up without any drugs."

Tiffany kept very still, although she wanted nothing but to shudder in revulsion.

"You know the rules—don't touch them until they're clean of dragon spawn."

Jones grunted. "What the others don't know won't kill them."

The other male's voice was firm as he said, "No. Break the rules and you'll be taken care of. Another night won't kill you."

"Fine."

The door shut again, and Tiffany heard the footsteps retreat.

Sitting up, she held the rope and hesitated a moment.

Not because of fear—no doubt she'd be processing this entire experience later when she wasn't pumped full of adrenaline—but rather at the two men's words.

Apparently, there were rules about kidnapping women pregnant with half-dragon-shifter babies and then forcing them to marry against their will.

To have rules in place meant that it happened often. The question was just how widespread it was.

Holy hell. Somehow, someway, she'd have to get David and maybe Wes to try and help free any others.

But for the moment, Tiffany focused on herself. After all, if she didn't get free, no one would know of the underground kidnappings and forced marriages.

She tied the rope to the bed frame and then went to the door, pressing her ear against it, listening for any sound.

A door shut somewhere, and something like the sound of a shower hummed down the hall.

Leaning back, she surveyed the area and slowly put her plan into action.

The dresser was easy enough to move with a few shoves, the carpet thick enough to hide any sound.

Taking out a drawer in case she needed an extra object to break the window, she put it nearby. Then she fetched the towel she'd kept back from her rope making and cleared off the end table. Lastly, she tucked a water bottle in the front of her sports bra, just in case she wouldn't be found for days.

Everything in place, Tiffany breathed in and out a few times to calm her pounding heart. She only had one shot at this, and she couldn't fuck it up because of nerves.

Finally, as calmly as she could be under the circumstances, she picked up the small yet sturdy end table, took a step back from the window, and slowly started twirling around. She had no idea how strong the glass was, and she needed momentum to put some extra punch into the impact. Finally, she took a step at the right moment and closed her eyes just as it smashed into the window.

Glass shattered, the shutters banged open, and Tiffany opened her eyes. She nearly blinked, not sure she could believe it worked.

However, she quickly regained her wits. Tiffany wrapped her arm in the towel to break the glass at the bottom, tossed the rope, and just as she climbed out the window, someone pushed against her door. The dresser moved, but held.

For now.

Other sounds erupted inside the house, but Tiffany didn't care. She quickly scaled down, to the point her hands were raw from the speed, and reached a height where she could safely jump to the ground. Just as she turned to run, someone came around the corner of the house.

If they had a gun, she was done for. But she didn't linger to dwell on that fact and just took off, running as fast as she could.

A shot fired, but it whizzed past her.

She just made the tree line as another shot fired, and shouting grew closer.

Fuck, fuck, fuck. They were gaining on her.

She pressed through the trees, uncaring that the

branches and brush scraped her legs and arms.

Her original plan had been to find an area with cell service and then climb a tree.

But as men shouted, the sound of breaking branches behind her, she knew she'd have to find a tree where she could hide and worry about finding cell service later.

If she couldn't get far enough ahead, they might see her climb into the tree. But right now, it was all she could think to do.

Pushing her legs harder, she tried to gain what advantage she could, all while looking for a tree that had branches low enough for her to grab and swing upward.

Which was harder than should be, given how little of the moonlight streamed down in this part of the forest.

There. She finally spotted one that was a little younger than some of the others. She'd have to climb to the adjacent tree to get high enough to hide, but she'd risk it.

With a burst of speed, she jumped and grabbed the first branch, ignoring the sting of her raw palms. Using her feet to climb up the trunk, she managed to wrap her legs around it and then pull herself up.

Her legs burned from scratches and her palms throbbed with pain, but she didn't waste time worrying about it. The voices were growing closer, meaning her window of opportunity was closing.

So she pushed herself to keep climbing up, up, up, as far as she could.

Just as she was about to reach out to a branch from the adjacent tree, she heard it—the roar of several dragons.

Tiffany wanted to sigh in relief, but the men's voices were nearly upon her, as were a few flashlights. The dragons might be close, but not close enough.

She reached over and nearly lost her footing. But she regained her balance and leaped to grab the branch of the next tree.

While it bounced dangerously, it held. And so she drew on her waning strength to pull herself up and climb farther up into the trees.

When voices were nearly upon her, she stopped and hugged the tree trunk, hoping she was high enough that they couldn't see her from the ground due to the nearly pitch darkness this far away from civilization.

She couldn't make out the murmurs below, and all she could do was wait.

Tiffany tried to adjust her footing to be more secure, but that's when she noticed the water bottle teetering on the edge of her sports bra.

She'd brought it as a precaution, trying to be prepared. And now, it could ruin everything.

She reached for it, but it was too late. The bottle fell, bouncing on the branches on the way down, and the men suddenly went quiet.

Eyeing the surrounding trees, she wondered if she could somehow move away from the men without going back to the ground.

However, before she could fully commit to a new plan, men shouted below, and sounds—shouts, shots, and roars—of a fight erupted below.

Her heart thumped, and she wondered if it could really be true. Had David and the others found her?

Then the phone in her bra buzzed and she nearly jumped. She yanked it out, flipped it open, and answered in a whispered, "Hello?"

"This is Maya. David and the others are either near you or at your location. Hang tight."

She closed her eyes but willed her body to hold out for a little longer. The last thing she needed was to faint and fall out of a tree. "I'm in a tree. High up in a tree."

"Stay there for now. We have your location, so once they're able, someone from the rescue team will help get you down."

"Okay," she whispered.

Maya hung up the phone, and Tiffany hugged the tree trunk tighter.

David was probably somewhere below her.

So close, and yet so far.

But as the shouting died down, she still worried. The human men had guns, after all.

No. She hadn't come this far to give up hope now. David would be alive. He just had to be.

Chapter Eleven

As soon as Tiffany's cell phone had reappeared on the tracking program, David had joined the team heading in her direction.

It hadn't taken long to find an isolated cabin on a large track of forest. From the air, they'd surveyed the trees until they'd seen a group of men rushing through it, toward something before stopping to look up.

Thanks to his keen dragon-shifter eyesight, he and the others had noticed the guns. Finding a big enough clearing to land and shift, they'd done so in a row until there were enough Protectors in human form to go and head to the suspicious group of humans.

David led them, doing his best to draw on his anger and push aside his fear.

The phone signal didn't necessarily mean Tiffany was still alive. But he hoped she was.

His dragon said, *She's smart. I'm sure she'll find a way to keep safe until we find her.*

I hope so, dragon.

They approached the humans, and David made a motion for them to move slowly. Once they were visible, he raised his fist to make the others stop so he could assess the situation.

There were about ten men, ranging in age from late teens to fifties, most of them armed in some way.

One was studying the ground, another asking which way she'd gone, and another looking up at the trees.

Then a water bottle bounced down through the branches of a tree and hit the ground.

They shouted, and David quickly noticed something moving in the branches above. However, when one of the men said, "The bitch is up there. Sorry, Jones, but it's now shoot to kill."

Before anyone could say anything else, David made the motion for them to attack, and he and the four others rushed from the undergrowth.

Speed was on the dragon-shifters' side, and David tackled the male pointing a gun up into the trees. Just as he rammed into him, the gun went off, and David knocked it out of the male's hand. The human tried to elbow him in the gut, but David moved to the side and punched him in the head. The male went limp, although still breathed.

His dragon sighed. *Pity.*

We need information, which means keeping them alive.

For now.

Ignoring his beast, he went to another male trying to climb the tree. David caught his ankle, yanked him down, and swung his fist into his jaw. The male grunted but then managed to get his bearings and tried to punch back.

It would be easy enough to extend a talon and slice through the male's belly, but David resisted. It was more than information keeping the enemies alive. He didn't want to find Tiffany, only to lose her again because he was sent to jail for murder.

However, he had no qualms about sending two quick jabs to the male's kidney and then clocking him out cold with an uppercut.

Two down, and he glanced around to see the other four dragon-shifters had taken care of the others.

Just then, Jon, Maya, and a few other of his clan members rushed into the spot. With the immediate threat under control, he turned to Maya. "Where is she?"

The dragonwoman looked at the phone in her hand and frowned. "She should be here."

A rustle from up above, and David knew. He shouted, "Tiffany?"

"David!" she shouted and then tried to cover a sob.

The sound tore his heart in two.

"Stay there. I'm coming."

With speed he didn't know he possessed, David rushed his way up the branches until he could just see her a few feet above. He met her gaze, took in her cuts and bruises, and resisted growling.

After he took care of his female, he'd deal with those who had frightened and hurt her.

He finally reached the branch just below her. His female was brave, but she looked exhausted and about ready to fall over. Keeping his voice gentle with the hopes of keeping her calm, he said, "Can you come down to my hand, love?"

She nodded, and as she sat on the branch and reached for him, he noticed her raw, bleeding palms.

Both man and beast nearly snarled.

But her voice caught his full attention. "Just take me home, David. Please?"

He nodded and gently guided her into his arms. He wanted to hold her, kiss her, and check her over, but the branch he stood on creaked a little. So he gently stroked her hair and said, "Put your arms around my neck and legs around my waist. I just need you to hold on until we reach the ground, love. Can you do that?"

She nodded and merely followed his instructions. And that made him suspicious.

Had they hurt her? Raped her? What had they done to his female?

His dragon said softly, *Let's get her home first. Then we'll take care of her.*

After gently stroking her back, David said, "Let me know if you can't hold on, Tiff."

She nodded, and he somehow forced his brain to focus on getting them out of the tree instead of wanting to find out why she was so quiet with him.

He didn't think she'd blame him for this. But maybe it was his fault. He'd left the clan before he'd mated her, which had made her vulnerable to ADDA's whim.

His dragon said, *Stop it now. We had no idea the League had ADDA employees working with them.*

Still, I should've protected her.

We'll talk more about this later.

David had one close call with a branch cracking, giving him just enough time to get to the one below, but he eventually made it to the ground. Once his feet touched the earth, he wrapped an arm under Tiffany's ass and another around her back to hold her in place.

He stood a few seconds, his eyes closed as he breathed in her scent and let his brain recognize his female was alive and safe.

Only when Jon spoke did he open them again. "A car is on the way, and Maya called Ashley. ADDA wants some of us to stay here until they can interview these bastards."

Tiffany spoke for the first time since the tree. "ADDA has people working with them. Don't trust them."

He stroked her hair and said, "These are people Ashley recommended, so they should be safe. Are there other ADDA people involved with what happened?"

Tiffany never lifted her head from his shoulder as she answered, "If so, they'll be in that house back there."

Jon signaled some of the Protectors to check it out and then turned back to David. "If we head back toward the clearing, there are some satchels with supplies to treat Tiffany's injuries."

No one may have checked her out yet, but they could all smell her blood from the cuts.

David whispered to her, "Do you have any serious injuries?"

She shook her head and then stopped. She moved her mouth to his ear and said barely audibly, "I don't think so. Although they…they talked about ending my pregnancy. So a doctor will have to check."

The thought that the humans hurt his female and had tried to take away his child caused a wave of anger he'd never known to course through his body.

If not for his female needing him, he'd hurt the humans tied up further.

His dragon said, *Tell her.*

He put his mouth at her ear. "You still carry our babe. I can smell my scent mixed with yours."

She let out a sob, and he held her closer against his chest. Making soothing sounds, he took her away from the area and toward the clearing. "It's all right, love. You'll be home soon enough and safe once more. No one will hurt you again."

Maybe some would think it a false promise, but David meant every word. No matter what it took, he'd protect his female from any other harm.

He murmured how brave, and smart, and resilient she'd been on the way to the clearing. Once there, he gently set her down on a rock, kneeled before her, took her face in his hands, and stared into her eyes. She was trying her best to be brave, but the exhaustion and resigned expression told him that everything she'd gone through was finally settling into her brain.

As he stroked her cheeks with his thumbs, he murmured, "Tell me where it hurts, love, and I'll fix you up."

She swayed for a second before putting out her palms. He retrieved the medical kit and did what he could to clean and bandage the wound.

Most everything else were light scratches.

Tiffany remained silent the whole time, but he hoped it was more from tiredness than anything else.

No. He wouldn't think about how she could decide he was too dangerous, too weak, unable to protect her, and any other number of faults right now.

So he merely scooped her up, sat down, and held her close as they waited for a car to get near enough.

She soon fell asleep, and David laid his cheek against the top of her head, breathed in her comforting scent, and realized how much she meant to him.

The thought of losing Tiffany forever made him want to scream. She brought light into his life and fun and simply made him a better male.

Maybe she wouldn't forgive him for what had happened over the last day. But no matter what she said or did, David would always love his human.

Which meant he had to find a way to convince her of it and to give him another chance to be the strong dragon male she needed.

Chapter Twelve

Tiffany opened her eyes to bright sunlight and instantly closed her eyelids again, rolling onto her side.

Her entire body hurt, her stomach rumbling in hunger, and yet she didn't want to get up from the cozy, warm bed.

However, a familiar woman's voice filled her ears, "You're finally awake."

Opening her eyes again, she focused and spotted the dark-haired, brown-skinned form of her boss and friend, Tasha Harper. She sat in a chair next to the bed with a book in her hands. Tiffany tried to reply, but her throat was so dry, and all she could manage to croak was "Water."

Tasha quickly helped Tiffany into a seated position and put a glass of water to her lips. While she hated being so weak, her arms protested from merely moving, and Tiffany didn't think she could hold the glass without spilling it.

Once she'd finished the water, Tasha set the glass down and studied her a beat before her lips twitched as she said, "It must be some sort of initiation for the human women here, to survive some kind of ordeal before mating their dragonmen."

Since Tasha had been shot at and her former bar in Reno targeted by the League before mating Brad Harper, it wasn't an odd statement.

Tiffany sighed. "Let's hope it doesn't happen again. Twice should be enough."

Tasha placed her hand on Tiffany's forearm and squeezed. "It might be easier going forward, I think. After all, we now know about the League infiltrating the local ADDA offices. Ashley knows the main person in charge of the branch. Give her a few weeks, and it'll be cleaned out, I'm sure."

As much as she was glad to see her friend, a certain dragonman's absence was stark. "Where's David?"

"Between setting up more patrols, finalizing a formal alliance with PineRock, and helping ADDA to interrogate those who took you, he's been rather busy."

She frowned. "How long was I out?"

"A little over two days."

She blinked. "That long?"

Tasha shrugged. "It's not every day you get

kidnapped, escape, and climb up a big-ass tree. Oh, all while pregnant, of course. Your body needed the rest." Her voice softened. "You're safe now, Tiffany. I hope you know that. A lot of people will tell you that, and it'll take some time for it to sink in, but if David is half as protective as Brad—which I think he will be, given how dragonmen act with their mates—no one will so much as sneeze on you without being tossed across the room."

Maybe some women would sigh and start crying, but Tiffany wasn't that person. True, she'd done it with David when he'd rescued her, but it'd been a trying set of days at that point. Not to mention she seemed to let her walls down around the dragonman too.

Although she had a sense the man would go in the opposite direction. "I know. But honestly, I'm more afraid of David and how he'll act now."

Tasha raised an eyebrow. "The clan leader curse bullshit?"

She blinked. "Does everyone know about it?"

Tasha shrugged. "Well, Brad talks with his sister, who is mated to David's cousin, so it comes up sometimes."

She sighed. "We were doing so well, and now I'm afraid it'll ruin everything."

"Just don't let it. David may be clan leader, but I think you've proven you have gumption and courage to match or nearly match his. Use it."

"Easier said than done."

"What happened to the woman who didn't hesitate to kick a man in the balls if he tried to grab your ass in the bar?" She touched her arm again. "Dragon-shifters are stubborn. Just be more so, and it'll be fine." She retracted her hand and smiled. "Besides, I'm not about to give up the only other human woman on StoneRiver. Call me a little selfish, but it's nice to have company. Especially when it's a woman with as much intelligence and strength as you. I don't suffer fools, and you're far from it, Tiff."

She snorted. "No, thank goodness." She searched Tasha's dark brown eyes. "Thank you. I think sometimes I need a verbal butt kicking."

"We all do." She stood. "I'm supposed to let everyone know when you're awake."

"Will you come back?"

Tasha shook her head. "No, I need to head to the bar. But either Megan or Justin will be along. However, I'll visit again when I can."

As her friend left, Tiffany settled against the pillows and thought about how she could convince David that her kidnapping hadn't been his fault. The dragons relied on ADDA for many things, and there had been no reason to suspect they'd work with the League.

However, she didn't think her dragonman would see it the same way. Which meant Tiffany was going to have to out-stubborn a dragon-shifter. And not just any dragon, but a clan leader to boot.

Yet with her future at stake, she was going to succeed if it killed her. When David had come to rescue her, and she clung to his body as he descended, she'd known that he was the key to the future she wanted.

And since she loved the damn man, she'd have to make sure he didn't push her away to try and protect her.

DAVID FINISHED his meeting with Wes and Ashley and slowly made his way toward his cottage, where Tiffany was resting and being guarded by two Protectors at all times.

Maybe it was overkill, but he didn't care. ADDA promised to look into it—at least those Ashley had trusted and spoke with—but his own trust had been shattered by recent events.

His dragon spoke up. *She's safe. The clan as a whole is angry at Zed's betrayal, and they're helping to look after our female.*

Well, at least those still here.

A few others had disappeared the same night Zed had. While David and PineRock were keeping an eye out for them, it wouldn't be the first time some dragon-shifters had snuck away to join another clan or hide out in the wilderness.

His beast replied, *Good riddance. If they can't see beyond their bias against humans, they have no place here. Tiffany is ours and part of the clan too.*

Or at least soon, he hoped.

David had done his best not to take the entire blame for what had happened. Not to mention Wes and Ashley had tried to convince him of it too.

And yet, he still felt like he should've done more.

Before his dragon could argue further, David reached his cottage, nodded to Maya and the other Protector on duty, and entered his house.

Music drifted from the kitchen, and he moved toward it. Stopping in the doorway between the hall and kitchen, he watched as Tiffany sang off-key and did something that resembled dancing as she scooped cookie dough onto a baking sheet.

For someone who was good at being active, she lacked any sort of rhythm.

He'd expected her to be recovering in bed or maybe resting. To see her dancing and singing was almost normal.

She must've sensed his presence because she turned around and smiled at him. Despite the scratches on her face and the smudge of flour on her cheek, he sucked in a breath at how beautiful she was, both inside and out.

But then his cynical side wondered if she was

trying to cover up the trauma she'd experienced and merely pretended everything was just fine.

His dragon sighed. *Talk with her and stop guessing.*

Knowing his beast was right, he walked toward her until he could gently wipe the flour off her face with his thumb. "You're awake."

She smiled up at him. "Yep, and extremely hungry. I've decided that as long as I'm pregnant, I'm going to eat what I feel like and not worry about it."

"You should always eat what you want." He traced her cheek, her brow, down her nose, and then gently took her chin between his fingers. "How are you?"

She raised her brows. "I'm doing as well as can be expected. Don't start treating me like I'll break, or it'll drive me crazy."

He frowned. "You were kidnapped, injured, and nearly killed. Not to mention you had to worry if they'd taken our baby or not. I think I'm justified in asking if you're okay."

She wiped her hands on her apron before taking his face between them. As her thumb caressed his cheek, David resisted sighing and leaning into the touch, needing to solely focus on her answer. She stated firmly, "I'm doing fine right now. I'm sure at times the experience will come back, and maybe I'll have nightmares. I don't know. But right here, right now, with you, in my kitchen smelling of chocolate chip cookies, I'm more than fine." She leaned against him, the heat of her body helping to ease his worry a fraction. "I need you to believe me, David. Tell me you do."

As he searched her hazel eyes, he replied, "I do. But I still worry."

She nodded. "I know. You're a clan leader, so it's sort of your job. But I survived. I'm the warrior queen, remember? With even more training, I could take down a group of armed men and flee all by myself."

He held her tighter against him. "Don't even joke about that."

She kissed him gently before pulling back. "It was a one-time fluke. Besides, now that the experience is over with, we don't have to worry about your curse. I'm not dead, which shows you that I'm made of sterner stuff."

Stroking her lower back, he murmured, "I want to believe that, but you may be an even bigger target now than before. Especially since you exposed the underground grab and marry operation by the League."

"I don't want them to rule our lives forever, but for now, I can stay on StoneRiver and maybe do something like coordinate activities for the children? Or maybe even the adults? I need something to keep me busy, or I'll be making dozens of cookies a day, and you'll soon have to roll me out the front door."

His frown finally eased as his lips twitched. "You

may be roll-worthy when you're nine months pregnant, but I doubt it before then."

She lightly smacked his shoulder. "You're supposed to say I'll be glowing and lovely and nicely rounded. Not that you're going to roll me out the door."

He chuckled, holding his female closer. "You know just how to ease my worries without even trying. I love you, Tiffany."

He hadn't meant for the words to come out, but he didn't regret them. Especially not as her eyes warmed, and she hooked her still-bandaged hands around his neck. "I love you too, David. Occasional grumpiness and all."

David burned to kiss her, and so much more, but he hesitated. She'd been through so much.

Tiffany rolled her eyes. "I'm not going to break."

And she closed the distance between them, her lips meeting his, and her tongue stroked for entrance.

He easily opened and pulled her against his body as he caressed her tongue, loving her taste, knowing he'd never tire of the female in his arm.

His hands moved to her ass and lifted. Without a word, she wrapped her legs around his waist. The instant her center pressed against his erection, he hissed.

His female broke the kiss long enough to whisper, "I think we have too many clothes on."

David wanted to say they should wait, but she

rocked against his hard cock, and reason flew his mind. The doctor had said Tiffany was fine, and his female had reinforced it. He'd just have to trust it was enough.

His dragon growled, *It is. Now, claim her so we can both be reminded she's here, and ours, and we're never letting her go.*

Moving toward the nearest counter, he sat her on it. Extending a talon, he shred her shirt and then her sweatpants. Another flick and her underwear was gone.

She moved to take his shirt, but he stepped back and tore it off. His jeans and boxers followed.

However, instead of immediately stepping between her thighs and thrusting home, he traced her cheek, down her neck, and to her breast. As he strummed her nipple, Tiffany groaned and put her hands behind her on the counter to steady herself. Unable to resist, he took her other nipple into his mouth and suckled.

Needing to touch him, she moved her hands to dig her nails into his hair, pressing him closer. Taking his time, he licked, nibbled, and suckled until his female squirmed on the counter, her arousal filling his nose and making his cock hard as stone.

Releasing her taut peak with a pop, he kissed his way down, taking an extra second to kiss her lower abdomen, until he kneeled between her thighs.

Looking up, he saw the mixture of desire, heat, and love in her eyes.

Never breaking his gaze, he licked her center, and Tiffany groaned. One taste of her sweet honey wasn't enough, so he licked and lapped and plunged his tongue into her pussy, loving how each sound told him how close she was.

He finally removed his tongue and moved to her clit, suckling it gently before lightly biting, and Tiffany arched as she screamed.

When she finally slumped a little, he took a few last laps to savor her orgasm before kissing his way up her body until he could take her lips in a long, lingering kiss.

A few beats later, her hand found his cock, and she whispered, "Take me, David. I need you inside me right now."

He positioned his dick and thrust to the hilt. Tiffany immediately wrapped her legs around his waist and dug her heels into his ass.

For a second, they merely stared at one another, no doubt both with heat, desire, and love shining in their eyes.

This gorgeous, funny, brilliant female was his. Forever.

Both man and beast needed more than gentle, and so he took her lips in a bruising kiss as he moved his hips.

Tiffany clung to his shoulders as David thrust as

if his life depended on it, needing to reach deeper and deeper, to feel her grip him as her warm heat surrounded his cock.

She dug her nails into his shoulders, and he moved even faster, loving how she groaned and moaned into his mouth, her hips meeting his every time, driving him closer and closer to the edge.

However, even with his orgasm hovering just out of sight, his female deserved to come first.

He moved a hand between them, lightly circling her clit in the way she liked until Tiffany screamed and convulsed around his cock. David thrust a few more times before he stilled, bliss exploding throughout his body, his female coming again all around him.

Once he finished spilling inside her, David held her close, his head on her shoulder, content to merely hold her and stroke her back.

He had no idea how much time had passed when Tiffany said, "That was almost as good as fresh baked cookies."

Leaning back, he snorted. "Good to know I rank just below cookies."

She grinned, and his heart skipped a beat. "Well, maybe better. Just a little." She kissed his jaw and whispered into his ear, "Although, since you set me on a counter away from all my cookie stuff, saving me from making more, I think you get bonus points for that. Cookies and sex. Hm. Maybe I should make that a regular thing."

He chuckled and kissed her nose. "I'll just have to try harder to rank even further above your baking then."

She wiggled, and his semihard cock decided to wake up again. "You could try to convince me again right now. Since I don't have anything in the oven, the house won't burn down if you decided to be extremely thorough in showing me why sex with you ranks above cookies."

He nipped her shoulder, and Tiffany laughed. He murmured, "Minx."

She looped her arms around his chest. "As long as I'm your minx, that's all that matters."

He whispered, "Always," before kissing her again.

And then he spent a few more hours convincing Tiffany that sex could indeed rank above cookies, treasuring the mate he'd thought would be his weakness but had ended up being both his greatest joy and source of strength.

Epilogue

Months Later

Tiffany looked from one newborn son in her left arm and then to her other on the right side.

She could barely keep her eyes open after the long labor, but David had his arms around her, helping to support the slight weight of their children.

Her mate kissed her hair and said, "I know at some point we'll have to stop staring, but I can't bring myself to do it right now."

She leaned her head against his chin. "Me, either. Although, all too soon we're going to have a handful."

He chuckled and then lightly stroked the back of her hands, the ones he had covered with his own.

"You have more energy than almost anyone I know. I think it's fate that you had twins to keep you on your toes."

"Or maybe it's to help us catch up to Justin and Megan."

David chuckled before kissing her cheek. "Four children is a lot. Let's see how we do first with two." He touched one son. "Adam." And then the other. "Griffin. Try to behave for your mother, okay?"

Griffin squirmed a little, but Adam merely slept.

Tiffany couldn't stop smiling. "I think Griffin is going to take after me, and Adam after you. So maybe there will be balance in the household."

He chuckled, and Tiffany merely leaned against her mate, loving how his mere presence gave her the strength to stay awake.

And although the pain and exhaustion from birthing twins were fresh in her memory, Tiffany secretly longed to try again for a daughter. One she could pass David's family heirloom—a beautiful silver comb—to when she was old enough. Maybe a daughter could even wear it on her mating day, like Tiffany had done.

Of course that was the future. She had two sons and a mate to love and cherish for now, and it was more than enough to make up for losing the one brother she'd probably never see again.

No. She pushed the thought aside. Today was happy, and it was Mark's loss, not hers.

As if sensing her thoughts, David nuzzled her cheek with his own, and she sighed in happiness. David would always be at her side, and her heart brimmed with love for her dragonman.

There was a knock on the door and her sister-in-law Gabby poked her head inside. "Can we come in? The doctor said it was okay as long as you weren't too tired."

She nodded. "For a short while. Then I'm going to need to sleep."

Gabby grinned as she entered with Ryan right behind her. "I was exhausted with one baby. I can't even imagine two at the same time. Although I'm going to have to get used to having two children soon enough."

Tiffany watched as Gaby glanced at her mate. She'd only recently told them all she was expecting another child.

And she was glad. Tiffany had only had her brothers growing up, and she wanted her children to be surrounded by a large, extended family.

Next, Justin, Megan, and their children also came in, all cooing over Adam and Griffin. While she wanted to hold her sons forever, she let everyone take a turn while David sat next to her and held her close.

She glanced up at him. He kissed her lips gently and murmured, "I love you, my queen."

Smiling, she replied, "And I love you too."

As they stared at one another, Tiffany was glad

she'd taken the chance with the dragonman at her side. One kiss had changed her life, but in the best way possible.

Together, they were making the clan stronger and forging a new path for StoneRiver. No more worries about curses, or hatred of humans, or any of those things.

She and David were crafting the best future possible for them and their sons. And nothing would stop them as long as they were together. Nothing.

Author's Note

I hope you enjoyed David and Tiffany's story! This tale has moved us closer to meeting the remaining two dragon clans in the greater Tahoe area— SkyTree and StrongFalls. There will be one more story set on StoneRiver before we move to one of the other clans. (I won't know which one until I write Tahoe #6…I don't plot my stories they just come to me.) And as a hint, one of the remaining clan leaders is interesting for their rarity…

The next Tahoe Dragon Mates story will be out in 2022. It will involve Jon Bell—StoneRiver's head Protector—and Cristina Juarez, the head Protector of PineRock. While the title isn't set in stone, I'm leaning toward *The Dragon's Rival* at the moment. It's the first time I'll have two dragon-shifters as the main couple for this series. The two have never met in person before, and let's just say that sparks will fly with these two…

And now I have some people to thank for getting this out into the world:

- To Becky Johnson and her team at Hot Tree Editing. They always do a fantastic job.
- To all my beta readers—Sabrina D., Donna H., Sandy H., and Iliana G., you do an amazing job at finding those lingering typos and minor inconsistencies.

And as always, a huge thank you to you, the reader, for either enjoying my dragons for the first time, or for following me from my longer books to this series. Writing is the best job in the world and it's your support that makes it so I can keep doing it.

Until next time, happy reading!

Also by Jessie Donovan

Asylums for Magical Threats

Blaze of Secrets (AMT #1)

Frozen Desires (AMT #2)

Shadow of Temptation (AMT #3)

Flare of Promise (AMT #4)

Cascade Shifters

Convincing the Cougar (CS #0.5)

Reclaiming the Wolf (CS #1)

Cougar's First Christmas (CS #2)

Resisting the Cougar (CS #3)

Kelderan Runic Warriors

The Conquest (KRW #1)

The Barren (KRW #2)

The Heir (KRW #3)

The Forbidden (KRW #4)

The Hidden (KRW #5)

The Survivor (KRW #6)

Lochguard Highland Dragons

The Dragon's Dilemma (LHD #1)

The Dragon Guardian (LHD #2)

The Dragon's Heart (LHD #3)

The Dragon Warrior (LHD #4)

The Dragon Family (LHD #5)

The Dragon's Discovery (LHD #6)

The Dragon's Pursuit (LHD #7)

The Dragon Collective (LHD #8)

The Dragon's Chance / Sylvia & Jake (LHD #9 / Sept 2021)

The Dragon's Memory / Emma & Logan (LHD #10 / May 2022)

Love in Scotland

Crazy Scottish Love (LiS #1)

Chaotic Scottish Wedding (LiS #2)

Stonefire Dragons

Sacrificed to the Dragon (SD #1)

Seducing the Dragon (SD #2)

Revealing the Dragons (SD #3)

Healed by the Dragon (SD #4)

Reawakening the Dragon (SD #5)

Loved by the Dragon (SD #6)

Surrendering to the Dragon (SD #7)

Cured by the Dragon (SD #8)

Aiding the Dragon (SD #9)

Finding the Dragon (SD #10)

Craved by the Dragon (SD #11)

Persuading the Dragon (SD #12)

Treasured by the Dragon (SD #13)

Trusting the Dragon / Hudson & Sarah (SD #14, Jan 2022)

Stonefire Dragons Shorts

Meeting the Humans (SDS #1)

The Dragon Camp (SDS #2)

The Dragon Play (SDS #3)

Stonefire Dragons Universe

Winning Skyhunter (SDU #1)

Transforming Snowridge (SDU #2)

Tahoe Dragon Mates

The Dragon's Choice (TDM #1)

The Dragon's Need (TDM #2)

The Dragon's Bidder (TDM #3)

The Dragon's Charge (TDM #4)

The Dragon's Weakness (TDM #5)

The Dragon's Rival / Jon Bell & Cristina Juarez (TDM #6 / 2022)

WRITING AS LIZZIE ENGLAND

Her Fantasy

Holt: The CEO

Callan: The Highlander

Adam: The Duke

Gabe: The Rock Star

About the Author

Jessie Donovan has sold over half a million books, has given away hundreds of thousands more to readers for free, and has even hit the *NY Times* and *USA Today* bestseller lists. She is best known for her dragon-shifter series, but also writes about elemental magic users, alien warriors, and even has a crazy romantic comedy series set in Scotland. When not reading a book, attempting to tame her yard, or traipsing around some foreign country on a shoestring, she can often be found interacting with her readers on Facebook. She lives near Seattle, where, yes, it rains a lot but it also makes everything green.

Visit her website at: www.JessieDonovan.com